Final Dawn

The Thrilling Post-Apocalyptic Series

Season 3

Mike Kraus

To My Readers:

Thank you for taking this journey with me.
Without your support, Final Dawn would not be possible.
Thank you.

Sincerely,
Mike Kraus

When the end of the world arrived, it came not with a bang, as most had expected, but with more of a "pfft." As tens of thousands of nuclear warheads detonated across the globe, those who were unfortunate enough to be caught in the blast had their lives ended so quickly that all they registered was a small "pfft" sound as their bodies were vaporized in the course of a few tenths of a second.

With that "pfft," the world ended far more quickly than it had begun. What took six days to create took less than an hour to destroy, as well over ninety-nine percent of the world's population was wiped out in the firestorm.

In the years leading up to the end, countless storytellers imagined what the end of the world would be like, with some saying that if it all ended in fire, no one would know who fired the first shot. This wasn't entirely accurate. Technology had moved too quickly to allow for this sort of surprise ending. Before the first bomb was halfway to its target, most first and second world countries knew exactly who had sent it hurtling into space. This knowledge was of no consequence, except to send the few men and women in the top echelons of government into complete and utter panic.

The rich, poor, powerful and powerless all looked to the heavens together, watching the end of the world descend upon them. Each and every one of them, without exception, was helpless. Greed, influence and intelligence meant nothing as they all bowed to the power of the bomb.

Final Dawn: Season 3

Rachel Walsh | Marcus Warden | David Landry
9:17 AM, April 21, 2038

A light wind blew through the air and the smell of honeysuckle was interspersed with that of pine. Both scents were thick in Marcus's nose as he sagged back against a control panel inside the locomotive, staring blankly at the wall in front of him. Other smells joined that of the plants, coalescing into a dystopian symphony. Blood, sweat, gunpowder and earth were close at hand, flooding his nostrils. Marcus wasn't sure if it was the aroma that made him dizzy or the matter-of-fact way in which Rachel had answered his question.

Marcus had never met the infamous "Mr. Doe," but his invisible hand combined with Rachel's ominous descriptions left little to the imagination. Cold, calculating and merciless, Marcus instinctively knew that the man would show no mercy and accept only death. And here he was, finally, showing himself after weeks of struggle had passed, preparing to cut them down like wheat under a scythe. Seated in his helicopter, Doe was nigh-untouchable, and it would only be a matter of time before he found and killed them.

Another explosion echoed through the train, sending Marcus diving on top of Rachel and Sam to protect them. Rubble showered down over the train, along with bits of steel, iron and wood. Marcus peeked through the front of the train, looking at the crater that sat a hundred feet up where the track used to be. A ten-foot section had been blow out of the track by the powerful missiles of Doe's black craft which was slowly drifting back down towards the train, no doubt searching for the survivors.

A pounding from the bottom of the locomotive caused Rachel to jump, pushing away from the center of the floor where the noise emanated. A muffled voice followed the pounding and a square section of slats rattled under the blows. "Open the hatch! Hurry!"

Glancing up at the sound of the helicopter circling overhead, Marcus crawled to the center of the locomotive and slid a latch to the side. He pulled up on a small handle, revealing a hatch through the floor straight down to the ground. Bloodied and caked with dirt and grease, David smiled weakly as he saw Marcus and Rachel peering down at him. He held his good arm aloft, reaching to Marcus who grabbed him, pulling him through the hatch and propping him up against a console. Another explosion echoed from far behind the train, followed by an intense rocking of the locomotive. Rachel stood weakly to look out the window and spotted a plume of smoke and dust in the distance.

"He just destroyed the tracks behind us." Sitting down next to David, she looked at him and Marcus, her face pale from shock and exhaustion. "We're trapped."

Clutching his injured arm, David leaned his head back against the console and closed his eyes. "So much for that plan. It was a good one, though, except for when Doe found us."

"How did he find us, anyway?" Marcus kept his voice low. "It's pretty strange that he just so happened to come across us now, isn't it?"

David pushed at the skin around the metal in his arm, wincing in pain as he considered pulling it out. "I don't know; the only way he could have found us is if he intercepted a signal between us and the satellite. But I have safeguards for that on the computer. Whenever I'm connected, I have a reminder set to warn me to change frequencies, just for this sort of thing. I wouldn't have thought Doe would be able to break into it, but I guess he did."

Marcus was looking at the floor as David spoke, and his eyes widened. Without lifting his head, he swallowed hard and tried to keep his voice calm as he spoke. "Reminders? Like warnings on the computer?"

David nodded, grimacing as he pulled lightly on the shrapnel embedded in his arm. "Yeah, it's pretty hard to miss. That's why I don't understand how I could have let this happen. Ah, damn! This hurts!"

Rachel examined David's wound, though there wasn't much she could do about it without access to their supplies. Thankfully, they had unloaded most of their gear from the APC and put it in the train, but it was several cars back, with no easy way to reach it without being spotted by the helicopter. As she and David talked about the best way to get the metal out of his arm, Marcus's face contorted as he remembered when he was on David's computer in the back of the APC. *There were the satellite images, which were easy to download, but then there was that alert or something that appeared...*

Glancing up, Marcus saw that Rachel had taken her rifle off of her back and had laid it on the floor next to her, along with a spare magazine. He locked eyes with Sam for a moment and made a motion for him to stay still. Sam whined but obeyed as Marcus grabbed the rifle, turning to jump out the front of the train. David and Rachel didn't notice his movement until it was too late and he was sprinting forward from the locomotive. "What the hell; Marcus, what are you doing?" David shouted at him, but Marcus didn't turn around as he shouted back.

"Ending this!"

Once he reached the edge of the destroyed section of tracks, Marcus stopped and turned around. He held the rifle aloft over his head with one hand and the spare magazine with the other. A few seconds passed before the helicopter began moving toward him as Doe finally noticed him. With slow exaggerated movements, Marcus laid the rifle and the spare magazine down on the ground in front of him then raised his empty hands back over his head. Hoping that Doe had a way of hearing him, he took a deep breath and shouted.

Leonard McComb | Nancy Sims
9:45 AM, April 21, 2038

"Let me see if I understand you correctly."

Commander Pavel Krylov leaned back in his chair. A slightly incredulous expression graced his face, though he was fighting hard to try to believe what the woman across from him had just described.

"Your country developed a nanotech-based weapon that can think for itself. One of its first actions was to virtually destroy the world with nuclear weapons. It then proceeded to turn many of the survivors into some sort of abominations, though there are still some who haven't been turned or outright killed by nano-robots due to some sort of DNA... what was it?"

"Whitelisting."

"Oh yes, due to some sort of DNA whitelisting. Furthermore, one of the chief scientists who worked on this project is with another group on the other side of your country with some sort of weapon that you hope will destroy these nano-robots. However, in case that weapon fails, you want me to take this ship to the coast and use our nuclear weapons against the nano-robots.

Would you say that's a reasonably accurate summary of what you described to me, Nancy?"

Nancy sat quietly for a moment before nodding slowly. "That's about the gist of it, yes."

Commander Krylov smiled briefly and looked down at his notebook. Halfway through Nancy's story, he had pulled it out to start jotting down pieces of information she had given to him. Picking up a cup of coffee sitting on a nearby table, he took a long sip, flipping through his notes. Nancy watched on in silence, chewing on her lip as she waited to hear Krylov's verdict. With a sigh, he closed his notebook and set his coffee down before pushing a button on an intercom built in to the table next to him.

"Send in the cousins."

Looking back at Nancy, Krylov sighed again. "If it were just your word for all of this, I'd have you and your companion thrown off the ship without a second thought." Krylov paused and nodded slowly, running his tongue over his teeth. "But... well, you can hear for yourself."

Commander Krylov and Nancy sat together in silence for a few moments until a sharp knocking came at the steel door.

"Enter!" Krylov swiveled his head to look at the two men who walked through the doorway. Hats in hand, they gave the commander a nervous salute and took their seats in a pair of chairs that Krylov gestured toward.

"Nancy, this is Andrey Lipov and Sergei Usov. I want you to describe these 'swarms' you spoke of to them. If you would speak slowly, I would appreciate it, since their English proficiency is somewhat limited."

Nancy nodded and took a sip of water before starting. "I'm pleased to meet you, Andrey and Sergei. I'm not really sure where to begin, though..." Nancy looked at Krylov for some assistance.

"Just tell them what the swarms look like, what their behavior was and anything else that comes to mind about them."

"Well," Nancy took a deep breath, "they're silver in color, normally anyway, though my friends have seen them in blue, as well. They make this sort of buzzing sound, like a swarm of bees, but angrier. I first saw them right after—"

"Nancy, if you could just stick to the details on these swarms for now and exclude the other details, that would be preferable."

Nancy glanced between Commander Krylov, Andrey and Sergei, realizing what the look on Krylov's face was about. *His men don't know what happened... dear God, they don't even know their world is gone.* With a gulp, Nancy continued. "I first saw them at a farm, when they were just going by, seemingly hovering in the air above the ground as they went. They moved quickly, too, but they weren't aggressive towards me.

Later on, though, we started to see and hear about more aggression from the swarms, and we found a lot of human remains from their work, too."

Over the course of her brief description of the swarms, Andrey and Sergei's faces had gone pale. They murmured something under their breath as they crossed themselves, sitting in rapt attention to Nancy. Finally, when she finished, Krylov spoke up.

"Is what Nancy has just described to you an accurate description of what attacked the landing party?"

Quick nervous nods were Andrey and Sergei's only responses to Krylov's question. Sighing deeply, the commander waved at them, dismissing them from the room. They were both up in a flash, racing for the door and slamming it shut before another word could be spoken.

"Commander, what happened to those men?"

Holding his cup of coffee, Krylov tilted his head as he watched Nancy, holding his tongue for a moment before responding. "You know, Ms. Sims, this entire situation is quite extraordinary. And, frankly, I'm still not sure what to make of it. Two Americans on my ship telling me that the world ended and that they need my nuclear weapons to wipe out an infestation caused by a rogue computer." Krylov sipped the coffee, curling his lip at the lukewarm beverage. He set it to the side and sighed again. "There are protocols for such an encounter as this, you know. Technically, I am supposed to take you back to Moscow for an interrogation before we negotiate your release with Washington."

"But, Commander, you—" Nancy started to protest, but Krylov raised his hand to silence her.

"Calm down, Nancy. As I said before, you and your companion are fortunate that we had such a terrible encounter with these things you described, and that there were two survivors to corroborate your story."

"Commander..." Nancy leaned forward, pleading with Krylov. "Please, tell me what happened. What do you know about these things?"

Krylov shook his head. "Nothing, I'm afraid, and certainly far less than you do. We were on patrol when we detected massive disturbances on the surface. We lost all communications and the late Commander decided to send out two landing parties; one to an outpost in our country and one to a small village along the Strait in yours. Those two men you just saw were the only survivors of the landing party in your country. Our commander was part of it, and from what we heard on the radio and have been able to extract from Andrey and Sergei, everyone else was killed by those swarms, what you say are nano-robots."

Krylov turned his notebook over in his palm, musing about the events of the last few weeks. "Then, of course, we detected something on the surface. It had to have been the same things. They didn't follow us into the water for some reason; I've no idea why, though."

Several minutes of silence followed after Krylov finished speaking as both Nancy and he thought over the revelations shared by one another.

"So, Commander, where do we go from here?"

Rachel Walsh | Marcus Warden | David Landry
9:24 AM, April 21, 2038

"You win, Doe! I surrender!"

Hovering just a few dozen feet from him, the helicopter's rotor wash was blindingly powerful. Marcus turned his head slightly and kept his eyes closed as he waited for a response. Several seconds passed, and Marcus had nearly convinced himself that the next noise to come from the chopper would be the sound of a missile. So certain was he of his inevitable death that the crackle of a speaker made his heart skip a beat before it resumed its rapid pounding.

"Kick it away, then get down on your knees."

The voice was precise and calculated, and Marcus knew that the lack of emotion in the voice was not just because it was coming through a speaker. The man behind the voice showed no emotions, and even now he was the epitome of detachment. Marcus did as he was told, kicking the rifle in front of him several feet away. The cockpit of the helicopter was darkened and impossible to see into, but Marcus knew that the man behind it was watching every movement with a hawk's eye, looking for any signs of treachery.

"Where are the others?"

Marcus had counted on this question coming next and already had a response planned. Assuming that Doe already knew exactly how many of them were there and who they were, Marcus spoke carefully, doing his best not to contradict anything that Doe might have seen or heard.

"Rachel was in the armored car, and David's... somewhere. I'm not sure where, but his leg's under the train."

Another several seconds passed in silence. Marcus fought the urge to look away, keeping his gaze trained on the helicopter. Finally, Doe's voice came again.

"Get down on your knees and put your hands behind your head. If you move, I will kill you."

You'd be better off killing me now, you fool. Marcus lowered his head, interlacing his hands behind it as he dropped to both knees. The whine of the helicopter's rotors lessened as it descended to the ground, finally touching down. Marcus raised his head slightly and watched as a side door on the helicopter popped open. With the rotors still spinning, a man exited the side door. Keeping his head low, he walked forward toward Marcus, pistol in hand. Dressed in his ever-present suit and tie, Marcus's first sight of Mr. Doe was somewhat threatening, if not slightly amusing. Though there was no questioning the fact that Doe was not a man to be trifled with, seeing a man wearing a suit during the apocalypse wasn't something Marcus thought he'd ever see.

After he cleared the rotors, Mr. Doe straightened his back and raised his arm, keeping his pistol trained on Marcus. An all-black Walther, the cold steel matched the darkness of Doe's suit and tie to perfection, giving an appearance that wasn't just a coincidence. Intimidation was part of Mr. Doe's arsenal of weapons, but it was one that Marcus was far too tired to bother with caring about. Bruised, beaten and run down, Marcus was stretched to his limit. His physical condition, combined with feelings of shame and guilt over having lost control earlier and having led Mr. Doe straight to them, Marcus's mind was no longer capable of feeling intimidation.

"Your name is Marcus, correct?" Mr. Doe stopped a few feet in front of Marcus. He held the gun with an iron grip, his arm never wavering as it kept the barrel aimed directly at Marcus's left eye.

"That's right. Marcus Warden." Marcus blinked his eyes as he looked up at Mr. Doe, trying to wash away the dirt and dust that was still collecting there from the helicopter's downwash. "Do you mind turning that damned thing off?" Mr. Doe's eyes were cold and nearly black, and his expression didn't change at all while both he and Marcus were speaking.

"I'm afraid not, Mr. Warden. Tell me again; where are the others?"

Marcus started to remove his right hand from behind his head to point toward the APC, but stopped as Mr. Doe's index finger smoothly moved toward the trigger. *Shit*, Marcus thought, *this isn't going to be as easy as I thought.* He stretched his back, moving it left to right in exaggerated circles. The cold steel and wood grain pressed up against the small of his back had turned warm, making every second more uncomfortable than the last. Having secreted the pistol beneath his shirt and pants before exiting the train, Marcus felt bad leaving Rachel and David defenseless, but one pistol wouldn't be enough to stop Mr. Doe. *It won't be enough if I fail here, anyway.*

"I already told you, Doe. Rachel was in the APC. David's probably dead by now, based on him *missing a leg*."

"You don't seem very broken up about their deaths, Mr. Warden."

Marcus shrugged as best as he could given that his arms were raised above his head. "I barely survived the end of the world, then I got to deal with some sort of hell creatures, then I got to drive all up and down the eastern seaboard and you just tried to kill me. I really don't give a *fuck* about them, you or anybody else."

Marcus breathed heavily at the end of his rant, his chest rising and sinking quickly. *Was that too much?* Doe was eying him closely, not saying a word. *Shit, it was too much.* Marcus tensed his muscles, preparing to throw himself to the side and grab his gun. It was a fool's plan, but he was about to completely run out of options.

"Well then, Mr. Warden." Doe's arm dropped a half inch, the only sign of his lessened aggression. "If they're dead, and you clearly will know nothing about what they knew, then your usefulness is at an end."

Flames exploded from the end of Mr. Doe's pistol along with a sharp crack that rose above the sound of the helicopter blades. Fire burned through Marcus's shoulder and he fell forward, unable to stop himself from slamming his face into the dirt. He rolled as his body's momentum continued forward, screaming in pain as his injured shoulder was scraped and bent against the ground, making the pain nearly unbearable.

"You son of a bitch!" Marcus yelled, spit flying from his mouth. "Just kill me!"

Doe held the gun to Marcus's head. Now just a foot away, he was crouched down, staring directly into Marcus's eyes. "I suppose I owe you that much. Tell me something, though, before I do so."

Marcus said nothing as he gritted his teeth and breathed heavily, fighting the blood loss and pain in his shoulder.

"Which one of you was foolish enough to lead me to you?"

Leonard McComb | Nancy Sims
10:02 AM, April 21, 2038

Another knock on the door followed Nancy's question, preventing Krylov from answering. A young man ducked in and quickly saluted the commander before leaning over and whispering in his ear. Krylov's face remained neutral and he nodded at the man. Taking his coffee cup, he stood up and gestured for Nancy to do the same.

"Please excuse me for a few moments, Nancy. I need to tend to some urgent business. We'll resume our conversation once I return. Until then, if you'd like to visit your companion, I've been informed that he's conscious. Afonin will show you to the medical bay."

Krylov stepped past the crewman who had spoken to him and hurried down the hall and out of sight. Grigory Afonin beckoned for Nancy to follow him and spoke in a thick accent, stumbling over his words. "Please, if you follow me." Commander Krylov, to his credit, had nearly perfect mastery of English, and when he had spoken with Nancy, his accent was far less noticeable than any of the others on the sub.

"Please, watch your head." Afonin pointed to the low doorway as they stepped into the hall. Turning left, Afonin walked quickly and Nancy hurried to stay with him, distracted by the numerous sights and sounds around her. After taking on the two Americans, Commander Krylov had decided to forego any pretense of stealth. The skeleton crew had quickly returned the Arkhangelsk to full power, and though most of the submarine was devoid of activity, lights, fans and electronic devices of various shapes and sizes were all powered up for use.

The walk from the room where Nancy and Krylov had spoken to the medical bay took several minutes. When she and Afonin arrived, he opened the door and stepped aside, allowing her to enter. "Knock to leave," he spoke quickly, then closed the door behind her. Turning from the sealed hatch to the room interior, Nancy's eyes adjusted to the dim lighting and she made out the shape of a body resting on a slightly inclined bed. She ran to the side of the bed and grabbed the hand of the person lying down, knowing who it was before seeing his face.

"Leonard! Thank God; you're alive!"

Leonard's eyes were closed, but he opened them at the sound of Nancy's voice. His face was bruised from falling to the ground when he was shot, and he was pale, but he smiled regardless, happy to see Nancy once again. A light blanket was pulled up to his chest, and as Nancy looked down the length of the bed, she could see that the outline of his right leg stopped at the knee. Nervously she reached for the blanket to pull it up and see the extent of the damage for herself, but Leonard's hand stopped her. He grasped her wrist weakly, trembling, and spoke softly, his voice cracking.

"Please don't. I'm not ready."

Nancy nodded and sat down on a stool next to Leonard. Taking his hand in hers, she held him tightly, staring at him in silence. Leonard's breathing was ragged, though his heartbeat was strong, and Nancy could sense that he was fighting both the loss of blood and whatever drugs had been injected into his body to help dull the pain.

"I spoke to the commander of the sub, Commander Krylov, and told him what had happened."

Leonard blinked his eyes slowly a few times, then gave up fighting the urge to close them. "Did he believe you?"

Nancy shrugged. "I'm not sure. He brought in a couple of other people who apparently encountered the swarms. Before we could keep talking he had to leave, though he said he'd be back to finish our conversation later."

Leonard didn't reply for a moment and Nancy looked at him closely, wondering if he had fallen asleep. After a deep breath, he opened his eyes again and looked at her intently. "Do what you have to, Nancy. This sub is our last chance if Marcus and Rachel fail. Do whatever it takes to convince him of the truth."

"Truth shouldn't need convincing." A voice from behind Nancy startled her and she jumped up, turning around to see where it came from. "It's the truth, after all."

Commander Krylov stood in the doorway to the medical bay with another man behind him. They walked in and pulled up a pair of stools next to Nancy before sitting down. Nancy sat back down slowly, still keeping Leonard's hand held tightly.

"Nancy, I gather that your companion's name is Leonard. May I ask, sir, your full name for our records?"

Leonard blinked lazily, masking the speed at which his eyes flicked between Nancy, Krylov and the other man seated next to the commander. "Leonard McComb. Professional sanitation engineer, survivor of the apocalypse and in desperate need of whisky and a peg-leg."

Krylov laughed heartily at Leonard's gallows humor. "It's good to see you in high spirits! Our doctor was worried you weren't going to pull through, but you've proved both his skill and your determination to live."

Still grinning, Krylov took a small laptop computer from the man seated next to him and opened it, revealing the screen. On it was a set of open files, one of which was strangely familiar to Nancy, though she had trouble placing it at first.

"Do you recognize this information?" Krylov asked, holding the laptop closer for both Nancy and Leonard to view. Nancy looked at Leonard, trying to remember where she had seen it, when a memory returned to her and she suddenly realized what it was. "Where did you get that?"

Leonard coughed and spoke before Krylov could answer. "I'll hand it to you, Krylov; your men are quite thorough in their searches."

Nancy turned back to Leonard, her eyes wide as he continued, explaining the source of the data to Nancy.

"I grabbed the data stick from Rachel back at the armory, before things went to hell. I figured it would come in handy at some point, if we ever needed proof of what's been happening."

"Mr. McComb is correct, Ms. Sims. After his surgery, we found this data stick hidden in his belongings. After decrypting it, we were able to analyze the data in short order."

Krylov paused and looked at Nancy and Leonard for several seconds.

"Well?" Nancy said impatiently, tired of Krylov's delays. "What's the point?"

"The point is that it confirms our story." Leonard answered in Krylov's stead, who nodded solemnly in agreement.

"Correct again, Mr. McComb. What you shared with me, Ms. Sims, was frightening, and viewing this data just made it a thousand times worse."

"So... you're going to help us?"

"Protocol, Ms. Sims, requires that I return to port immediately and deliver this high-value information to our intelligence service." Krylov looked at the floor, sighing softly to himself. "However, given that there is no intelligence service, port or anything else left to speak of, I find myself forced into an awkward and unforeseen position."

"Commander," Leonard said, "what do we have to do to convince you to help?"

Krylov stood, closed the laptop computer and placed it under his arm. He took a deep breath, replaced the hat on his head, and straightened his back, adopting a more formal posture.

"Mr. McComb. Ms. Sims. The Arkhangelsk and her crew stand ready to aid you in the destruction of this pestilence."

Rachel Walsh | Marcus Warden | David Landry
9:30 AM, April 21, 2038

Movement from behind Mr. Doe caught Marcus's eye. Before he could stop himself, he glanced at it, though Mr. Doe didn't appear to have noticed thanks to the sweat, tears and dirt coating Marcus's entire face. Marcus felt his heart jump as he made out the blurry form of Rachel, who was slowly walking up behind Mr. Doe. Her footsteps masked by the sound of the helicopter, Rachel was armed with only a shovel, though even a momentary distraction was all Marcus would need to finish out his plan how he had intended.

"Hey." Rachel's voice was weak and strained. "Doe."

Mr. Doe turned quickly, whipping the pistol around to face the new voice behind him. Rachel was just a few feet away, though, and lashed out with the shovel. The metal end collided with Mr. Doe's left arm, knocking him off balance, though he still retained the pistol in his right hand. Unable to keep a grip on the shovel in her weakened state, it flew out of Rachel's hands, clattering to the ground far out of reach.

A cold sneer, the first—and last—sign of emotion in Mr. Doe came as he leveled his gun at Rachel. As he opened his mouth to speak at her, a shot rang out. Looking down at his hand, he immediately questioned whether he had inadvertently fired his weapon or not. His finger was not on the trigger, though, and the lances of pain in his back and chest verified that the shot did not come from his gun.

Three more shots rang out in rapid succession and Rachel dropped to the ground as two of the rounds passed through Mr. Doe's body, tumbling end over end out the other side. The final round passed through his heart, lodging in his ribcage, and sending him toppling to the ground. He fell flat on his face, like Marcus had done, but instead of trying to move or roll with the impact, he stayed where he had fallen.

Behind where Mr. Doe had been standing, Marcus was on his side, his gun still pointed at the body in front of him. His arm was shaking violently and his breathing was labored as the red stain on his shoulder slowly spread down his chest. As Mr. Doe succumbed to his wounds, his body gave a small shudder. In that same instant, the whine of the helicopter grew louder as it began to lift off from the ground on its own. Presumably controlled by an autopilot system linked to a dead man's switch on Mr. Doe's person, the helicopter rocketed away, though a distant explosion was heard a moment later, accompanied by a plume of smoke far in the distance.

Rachel and Marcus stared at each other over the body of Mr. Doe, neither of them speaking as they each caught their breath and tried to recover from what had just occurred. The sound of footsteps came from behind Rachel, who turned to see David slowly walking up on them, holding a piece of torn cloth against his arm. He stopped over Mr. Doe's body and examined it before nudging the corpse with his foot. Satisfied that Mr. Doe was finally dead, he leaned down and removed the pistol from Mr. Doe's death grip before sitting down next to Rachel and Marcus.

"Huh." David snorted as he looked at Mr. Doe's body. "That was sort of anti-climatic."

Marcus started to chuckle, holding his shoulder through the pain. "For you, maybe."

Rachel stood up and hobbled over to Marcus. She knelt down next to him and examined his shoulder. "It looks fairly clean. It passed right through, so you should be okay. We just need to clean it up and bandage it before an infection sets in."

David got up before Rachel and headed back to the train. "I'll be back with the medical kit in a minute."

Rachel nodded her thanks and watched him walk off, waiting until he was halfway back to the train before speaking to Marcus.

"It was you, wasn't it?"

Marcus looked Rachel in the eye, still feeling no small amount of shame over what had happened. "I didn't know, Rachel. I was just looking at the computer and something popped up. I can't even remember what it said at this point."

Rachel nodded slowly and patted his arm gently as she sat down next to him to wait for David to return. "I know you didn't know, Marcus. For the time being, let's keep it between you and me. David's already strained enough as it is about your… well, whatever it was that happened before. He doesn't need to know about this; it won't do him any good."

Marcus nodded and leaned his head back against the ground. The sunlight overhead was warm on his face, though the distant black clouds rolling in signaled that it wouldn't last for long. "I can't believe this guy's dead. I mean, really, I thought it'd take more than this to kill him."

Rachel sighed and stared at Mr. Doe's body. His suit was wrinkled, torn and marred with dirt and a red stain on the ground was slowly spreading as his blood flowed along the path of least resistance. "I think it's a rather fitting end, personally. After all he did and all I'm sure he was still trying to do, *this* will be his final resting place."

"Sorry it took so long; this was all I could find." David held up a clear plastic case filled with bandages, gauze, basic surgical tools and a small variety of medications. With a chunk of metal still embedded in his arm, he moved gingerly, not wanting to accidentally trip and drive the shrapnel further in. Rachel took the case from him and opened it, removing a pair of gloves, a small bottle of iodine, and several bandages and a roll of gauze. She motioned for David to sit next to her and then cleaned the area around the shrapnel, instructing him to keep his arm still despite the pain. After liberally dousing it with iodine, she gripped the shrapnel with her gloved hand and gently began to pull it out.

Rachel was by no means a medical professional, but her guess that the shrapnel hadn't penetrated far into David's arm was correct, and the metal was quickly out. Following that was more iodine and a quick wrapping of bandages to help minimize the bleeding. After tending to David, Rachel turned her attention to Marcus, though there wasn't much she could do for him except clean both sides of the wound, bandage him up and put his arm in a makeshift sling. With all of their immediate injuries cared for, they all walked slowly back to the train and climbed inside.

"So," David said at last, "What're we going to do now?"

Leonard McComb | Nancy Sims
11:48 AM, April 21, 2038

The energy on the command deck of the Arkhangelsk was electrifying. A hum was in the air, carried on the backs of the crew members who hurried back and forth as they prepared the ship for its most dangerous mission yet. Although the ship had an official top speed of forty knots, Commander Krylov had ordered them to increase it by a minimum of fifty percent in an effort to get to the gulf as quickly as possible. They could launch the missiles before reaching the gulf if they had to, but they would not be in radio range of the area for a few more days. Without radio contact with Rachel, Marcus and David, they would have no way of knowing precisely where to target the missiles, assuming they would have to use them at all.

"How can you be certain that your companions are still alive?"

Commander Krylov and Nancy were standing around a chart table in a corner of the command deck, poring over a map laid out in front of them. Seated next to them with a pair of crutches leaning up against the wall, Leonard raised himself up as much as he could in his chair to get a view of the map as he responded to Krylov's question.

"The last radio contact we had with them was before we hit Anchorage, but we got cut off, presumably because of the storms."

"Storms?" Krylov looked puzzled.

"Oh yes," Nancy answered, "these massive super storms. Haven't you seen them?"

Krylov shook his head slowly. "No, we haven't seen anything of the kind. But we haven't been on the surface much as of late. Once we detected those nano-robots on our scanners, I decided it would be wiser to stay submerged."

"Well, whatever they are, they're huge. They take days to pass by, and they're covering huge spans of surface area, with fairly short breaks in between them."

Krylov sighed and looked back at the map, running his index finger along a path that had been drawn and redrawn several times already. "Then we'll just have to make our move and hope that we can reach them once we get closer to the coast."

A shudder came from somewhere deep in the bowels of the submarine and Krylov stood straight, looking across the command deck at the face of a nervous crewman. He shouted at the crewman in Russian and a quick response came in turn. It had pleased Krylov, apparently, because his demeanor relaxed and he leaned forward on the table once again.

"The engines are now running at one hundred and fifteen percent. We'll be at one-twenty-five within the hour."

"Can this old thing handle that?" Leonard looked mildly concerned as he asked the question due in no small part to the ominous low frequency vibrations that were coursing through the vessel.

"The Arkhangelsk may be old," Krylov said, with a slight note of warning in his voice, "but she'll get us there. Right now we need to focus on what's going to happen once we breach the canal and reach the gulf."

Redesigned six years earlier, the Panama Canal had received a complete upgrade for the modern age. Twice as wide as it had previously been, the canal was nearly completely automated and its pumps operated off of a combination of geothermal and solar energy. The only human input required to pass through was to activate a control station, though the task was trivial compared to the larger goal. Once through the canal, the Arkhangelsk would have to travel as fast as her crew could push her to reach radio range with the area that Leonard and Nancy presumed Rachel, Marcus and David would be. Without direct communications with them, the crew on the sub would have no way of knowing if—much less where—they should be firing their missiles.

Leonard sat back in his chair and rubbed his eyes. "Just get us in radio range of Marcus and Rachel, Commander, and we'll be able to tell you exactly where to put the missile."

One of the command crew rushed to Krylov, a computer in hand, and placed it on the table. "Sir," he spoke, in English no less, "we were able to reach the satellite. We're getting live imagery now." Krylov tilted the screen of the laptop so that Nancy and Leonard could see. Images scrolled slowly through the screen, showing roiling storms over the western section of the USA.

"Wait a second, that's the satellite that Rachel and David were accessing." Nancy couldn't help letting the slightest bit of an accusatory tone slip. "How did you get this?"

Krylov held up the data stick they had taken from Leonard and placed it on the table next to the laptop. "Whoever put this together included access instructions for the satellite; it was designed that way, Ms. Sims. The person who made this wanted whoever found it to have full access to every resource left." Krylov pressed a button on the laptop and an image on the screen froze. "And it's a good thing, too."

A massive storm was sweeping in toward the coast, directly toward the Arkhangelsk's position. Looking across the bridge, Krylov shouted at the crewmen, raising his voice above the groans of the ship. "It's time to submerge, gentlemen. Take us to five hundred!"

Shouts of affirmation came back and the submarine began to tilt forward, racing downward at a steep enough angle that Nancy and Leonard both clung to the table with white knuckles. Krylov smiled at them, remembering what his first voyage on a sub had been like, and wondering what was going through the heads of the two American civilians who had found their way onto his vessel.

Rachel Walsh | Marcus Warden | David Landry
5:58 PM, April 21, 2038

After talking for a few minutes about what they were going to do next, Rachel, Marcus and David all fell asleep on the floor of the locomotive, their bodies succumbing to the effects of both their wounds and exhaustion. With the train tracks both ahead and behind the train destroyed, they had to quickly face up to the fact that they weren't going to be going anywhere. The destruction of the APC eliminated any hope of continuing on with it, as well, and the likelihood of finding any other vehicles nearby that would be in working condition was slim at best.

The first to wake up, Marcus quietly exited the train with Sam, walking slowly down the length of the train in the last few minutes of light they had. Night was nearly upon them, along with the edge of another set of storm clouds, and Marcus wanted to be certain that they hadn't missed anything. Flashlight in hand, he scanned the interior of the train cars, the doors of which were still rolled open from when the creatures inside had been trying to attack them.

Most of the contents of the boxcars were unrecognizable to Marcus, except for the few cars directly behind the locomotives. In addition to holding Bertha, the front few boxcars also held a variety of workman's tools, thick metal rails, wooden ties, spikes and—in the fourth car—a large amount of gravel for smoothing out uneven surfaces. While Marcus had seen the contents of a few of the boxcars previously, he had been under enormous stress while doing so, and this was his first chance to check them out in a relatively calm environment. Clenching his teeth, he pulled himself into the second boxcar, trying to keep his shoulder as still as possible.

Marcus played the flashlight over the interior of the darkened boxcar as Sam sniffed around his feet, growling at two dead creatures that were hanging out of the open door on the opposite side. Thunder rumbled in the distance, causing a shiver to run down Marcus's spine as the eerie atmosphere of the train began to affect him. Shaking the feeling off, he continued looking through the supplies, nurturing the seed of a plan that he had been forming since shortly after he had shot Mr. Doe in the back. Moving on to the next train car, he found that it was filled with more rails and ties, and between all of the supplies he had seen, there looked to be enough to lay down a half mile or more of track with little or no difficulty. From Marcus's estimation, the amount of track that had been destroyed in front of them by the missile was no more than thirty feet in length.

It'll never work, he thought, *but stranger things than this have succeeded so far.*

Walking back to the locomotive with Sam behind him, Marcus heard Rachel and David's voice before he saw them. As he rounded the corner to the front of the train, he saw the two of them standing near the destroyed section of rail, gesturing between it and the train behind them.

"Oh come on, David. It can't be that hard."

"Are you serious? One of those ties is several hundred pounds on its own. And none of us are in the best of shape, either."

The pair turned and looked at Marcus upon hearing the sound of gravel crunching underfoot. Smiling, he nodded toward the damaged track and spoke to Rachel. "So you had the same idea, eh?"

David threw his hands into the air and walked back toward the train in frustration. "You're both insane!"

Marcus watched David walk back to the locomotive and climb back inside before turning back to Rachel. "What do you figure our chances here are?"

"Based on our track record, I'd say we've got a pretty good shot. It's not like we have any other choice, though. Going on foot is a no-go, and finding a vehicle that's still operational that could hold Bertha is a fool's errand."

"So is trying to lay down thirty feet of railroad track when none of us have any idea how to do it."

Rachel gave Marcus a half-smile and walked a few feet forward, to the edge of where the track had been damaged. She wobbled slightly as she walked, and Marcus could see that she was still fighting through a large amount of pain. The shallow crater in front of her was several inches deep, down to the bottom layer of gravel that the railroad ties rested in. The major damage hadn't been to the ground, though, but to the ties and rails themselves. Pieces of the wooden ties were scattered around and in the crater, and several short sections of rail were missing as well. At both ends of the crater, where the rails were intact, there were a few feet of mangled, twisted steel loosely joined to the intact sections of rail by screw spikes.

"Come on now, it won't be that bad." Rachel patted Marcus's shoulder as she circled around him, walking the perimeter of the crater. "It's not like we have to make it perfect. If we can fill this hole in, get a couple of ties to put down in the middle and nail down a few lengths of rail on each side, we should be okay."

Marcus gestured to the long trail of train cars behind him. "Somehow I doubt that half-assing a railroad track is going to get that thing across."

"Well," Rachel mused, "what if we disconnected everything but the locomotives and the boxcar holding Bertha?"

Marcus kicked a large piece of gravel into the shallow crater, nodding as he considered Rachel's suggestion. "I guess that would be easier, but won't the AI be expecting a full train to arrive?"

"We'll burn that bridge once we come to it. For now, let's just see if we can do the impossible. Again."

Leonard McComb | Nancy Sims
4:18 PM, April 21, 2038

For what felt like the hundredth time in a day, Nancy was once again overwhelmed by the magnitude of the vessel she was on. Having been given nearly free reign to go wherever she wanted on the sub, she had taken to wandering the corridors while Leonard rested. Exploring the vast interior of the submarine was a strange experience for Nancy, who had never dreamed that a craft as large as the Arkhangelsk could have existed, let alone be capable of traveling at such incredible speeds underwater. After exploring the ship for a few hours, Nancy finally found her way back to the dining room, where half of the small crew—including Commander Krylov—were gathered for a meal.

Nancy walked slowly through the dining room until she caught Krylov's eye. He quickly waved her over and she sat down next to him. A moment later a plate of steaming food was deposited in front of her along with a drink, napkin and utensils. While the food was less than appetizing, she dug into it with gusto, having only had a few sips of water and military rations since arriving on the sub.

"How is Mr. McComb doing, Ms. Sims?"

Nancy wiped some crumbs from the corner of her mouth and cleared her throat. "He was sleeping when I checked in on him last. I was going to go bring him some food. I don't think he's had much at all to eat."

Krylov waved his hand dismissively at her. "No, no, he's being well looked after. The doctor is ensuring he's getting everything he needs. What about yourself? Was your exploration of the Arkhangelsk illuminating?"

Nancy nodded and laughed lightly. "It was nothing short of astonishing, Commander. It's like a city under the water. There aren't that many people, though. It looks like hundreds could fit in here."

"One hundred and sixty is the recommended complement, but she can hold far more, it's true." Krylov said. Nancy had finished eating and Krylov stood up, motioning for Nancy to follow him. They walked together out of the dining room down the hallway as Krylov continued to talk. "Of course, when we left port, we already had a small crew, but losing two landing parties to those things up there cut us down to what you see now."

Krylov's heavy sigh weighed on Nancy and she looked at him closely, noticing the dark circles under his eyes and worry lines etched into his forehead. "Have you ever taken command of a submarine before?"

"I'm afraid not." Krylov snorted. "I wasn't going to be up for a promotion for quite a long time. Losing Commander Alexeyev has been... difficult. On all of us. This nano-robot business, though, and the whole end of the world situation, that's going to be even harder to break to the crew."

"You mean they don't know about it?"

"Not all of them, no. A select few who I trust to be discrete have been informed. They're the ones who worked on decrypting the data stick and who accessed the satellite, among other things. The rest of the men don't need to know yet. Knowing that their country has been obliterated would do little to invigorate then for the journey ahead, and we'll need every man's full attention to see this through to the end successfully."

Nancy was quiet for a moment as she digested what Krylov had told her. When she spoke again, her voice was softer. "You said the country's been obliterated. Is that because..."

"Yes. As the satellite was passing over, I examined the imagery quite closely. We wouldn't be en route to your country if mine wasn't all but wiped off the face of the earth." Krylov's tone had a sting near the end, putting Nancy on the defensive.

"Commander, you realize that we were hurt just as much as you, right? I've seen more death and destruction than I could have ever imagined just in the few places we've been. You're not the only one who's suffered losses."

"No, Ms. Sims, we aren't. But we also aren't the ones who started this disaster." Krylov's eyes and voice started to fill with anger, though as he looked at Nancy it quickly died out. He sighed again and stopped, leaning against the wall in the empty corridor. "You have my apologies. You are no more responsible for this than I am."

Nancy placed her hand on Krylov's shoulder, smiling grimly at him. "There's no need for apologies, Commander. None of us expected to be in this situation. I, for one, am glad that we found you, and I know Leonard is as well. If Marcus and Rachel fail, then you and your crew are the last hope for all of us."

Krylov closed his eyes momentarily and nodded solemnly before pushing off the wall and continuing his walk. Nancy stayed next to him as they wound their way to the medical ward where Leonard was sleeping.

"If you'll excuse me, Ms. Sims, I need to tend to my duties. Please don't hesitate to call for someone if you or Mr. McComb need anything."

Rachel Walsh | Marcus Warden | David Landry
2:18 PM, April 23, 2038

Three strong individuals with experience, determination and a healthy dose of gumption could easily have replaced thirty feet of railroad track in far less than a day. Three inexperienced, injured and exhausted individuals struggling against all odds, though, took quite a lot longer. After consuming a healthy dose of painkillers that did little to diminish their discomfort, Marcus, Rachel and David set to work, committing to the only course of action open to them. The first few hours of the repair started with an argument between Rachel and David that lasted well into the afternoon. As Marcus slowly pushed load after load of gravel from the boxcars to the crater in a wheelbarrow he had found in a pile of other tools, he listened to Rachel trying to convince David that repairing the track was their only shot at getting out of their current predicament. David argued ferociously, citing their injuries, their lack of knowledge on the subject and listing off as many different reasons why it wouldn't work as he could think of.

Each argument was shot down by Rachel until, finally, Marcus ended the whole conversation by sticking his head in the doorway of the locomotive and whistling loudly.

"Hey, assholes. I got the hole filled in. Do you two want to come help, or would you rather dick around some more while I finish it all up myself?"

Initially, David wore an angered expression, at least until he glanced past Marcus to see a pile of gravel filling the shallow crater where Mr. Doe had destroyed the track. This combined with the fact that Marcus's arm was still in a sling broke David's resistance and his anger fell, replaced with equal parts shame and acceptance. For her part, Rachel was apologetic, having completely lost track of time as she had argued nonstop with David. Marcus waved them away, rolling his eyes as he slowly pushed a final load of gravel to its destination. Rachel and David joined him and, together, the three evaluated Marcus's work in the light of the electrical storm overhead. Over the course of the next day and a half, Rachel and David threw their backs into the work alongside Marcus. Remaining uncharacteristically quiet, David said nothing negative about Marcus the entire time, having gained a healthy dose of respect for the man that he had shown incredible disdain towards just a few days prior.

The end of the second day of work brought renewed hope to the trio as they sat around a small fire just outside the lead locomotive, rewarding themselves for their hard work with a night of rest. Marcus stroked Sam's back as the dog laid sprawled out in front of the fire, dozing with an expression of ecstasy on his face.

"How much more do you figure we have to go before it's done?" David's question was the most he had spoken since the end of his argument with Rachel. Looking at Marcus briefly, Rachel cleared her throat and took a sip from her bottle of water.

"I think we've done all we can for laying out the ties. That was a hell of a job, by the way; we should all be proud of that." Marcus nodded and smiled in agreement as she continued. "Now that the damaged ends of track are gone, we have to decide how to put down more of it. The way I see it, since we don't have nearly enough ties out there, we'll want to use the longer sections of track over the shorter ones."

"The disadvantage," Marcus interrupted, "is that they're much heavier and harder to handle than the shorter pieces."

"Exactly. So that's what we have to decide. I *think* the longer sections will offer us more stability when we actually try to get across them, but it's going to take a while to put them in. If we use the shorter sections without having more ties, though, then I think that has a much greater likelihood of falling apart when it comes time to test it out."

Rachel looked at David, whose gaze was transfixed on the flickering fire. "What do you think, David?"

David blinked several times and took in a sharp, quick breath as he looked up at her. "Sorry, what?"

"Are you all right, David?" Marcus put his hand out on David's shoulder, feeling the man pull away ever so slightly at the touch.

"Sorry, yeah I'm fine. Just distracted, that's all."

Rachel tilted her head and furrowed her brow. "What's going on?"

"Right now we have no way of contacting Leonard and Nancy, assuming they're still alive and made it to the sub. The only satellite radio uplink that I know of was in the APC, and that's long since gone."

"Doesn't the train have a radio of some sort?" Marcus resumed stroking Sam's fur, keeping an eye on David as he did so.

"I assume so, but that's just a standard high power transmitter. The range on that will be limited to a few hundred miles, if we're extremely lucky and can boost the power, too."

Rachel closed her eyes, imagining how far such a transmission range would get them. "Damn. That's a decent distance, but not very far."

"Especially when you're trying to coordinate a nuclear launch."

"Well," Marcus said, trying his best to be cheerful, "it shouldn't come to that, right? Bertha's going to make the need for more nukes something to not even worry about."

"One can only hope so." The dread and uncertainty that permeated David's words was lost on neither Marcus nor Rachel. As the group fell silent, Marcus lay back on the ground and closed his eyes. As he fell quickly to sleep, a thought tickled the back of his mind, making him feel even more nervous. If they couldn't reach Leonard and Nancy to tell them to launch the missiles, then they would also be unable to reach them to *keep* the missiles from launching.

Leonard McComb | Nancy Sims
1:22 PM, April 23, 2038

Nancy had not slept soundly for the last two nights in the medical ward. Despite the extra blankets and pillows provided to her by Commander Krylov, every time she closed her eyes, she couldn't help imagining the waters just outside the hull, pushing inward with a frightening amount of force. When she was able to sleep, it wasn't soundly, and she found herself waking at the slightest noises. While the normal disturbances were the creak of the hull, a crewman walking down the corridor or the doctor periodically coming to check up on Leonard, the latest agitation came from the sound of rubber tapping along upon metal.

Nancy opened one eye, searching the room to find the source of the noise when she saw Leonard's empty bed. Springing out of her cot, she looked frantically around the room to see where Leonard had gone.

"Whoa there! What's wrong?" Leaning up against a wall, Leonard had crutches under his arms as he balanced on one leg. He hobbled back towards her, moving slowly as he was still growing accustomed to this new way of getting around.

"You shouldn't be up!" Nancy rushed to his side and put her arm around him, but he shrugged her off, giving her a smile as she watched him walk around the room.

"It's okay, Nancy. I'm just getting used to these damned things. Are you all right? You jumped up pretty quickly there."

Nancy sank back down on the cot and held her head as she was overcome with a wave of dizziness. Leonard sat down next to her and leaned his crutches against the wall. They slipped almost as soon as he let them go, clattering to the floor out of reach. Leonard sighed and shook his head, laughing softly to himself. He patted his right leg gently, smiling at Nancy as she looked at him in concern.

"This sure has turned out to be one interesting trip we've taken. I have to say, though, that I didn't expect to lose a leg along the way."

Nancy started to smile but stopped, feeling bad about it the second the corners of her mouth started to turn upward. Leonard took her hand and grasped it tightly. "Don't be afraid to laugh, even in the face of all of this."

Nancy tried to force a smile as she stood up. "You really shouldn't be up and around right now... if you were in a hospital, they'd make you—"

"I'm not in a hospital, am I? Besides, I'm not going to be much use to you all if I'm lying around with my foot in the air. I'll be fine, I promise."

Leonard pushed himself up on his good leg and stood at the edge of the bed, one hand on the upper bunk as he watched Nancy closely. Tears welled in her eyes and ran down her cheeks as she felt overcome with sorrow for Leonard and the position they were in. Leonard held out his arms and she hugged him tightly, trying to fight the steady tide of emotion. A few moments passed in silence before she pulled away, only to have Leonard hold her shoulders and look her closely in the eye.

"We're almost done with this, Nancy." Leonard's voice was an island of calm stability. "Just hang on a bit longer."

The door to the medical ward slammed open and two crewmen rushed in, out of breath and with red faces. Nancy quickly wiped the tears from her eyes and collected the crutches from the floor, giving them to Leonard who tucked them under his arms. After taking a deep breath, the first of the two crewman tried to explain something to Leonard and Nancy, though a combination of poor language skills and having run nearly the full length of the ship made him difficult to understand.

"Commander! You come! Hurry!"

The two crewmen ducked back out into the hallway and resumed their run, their footsteps echoing down the corridor until they were heard no more. Nancy and Leonard looked at each other and Leonard shrugged and began to hop forward on his crutches. Nancy put out a hand to stop him but he shook his head and kept going forward, moving faster with each step he took. "It sounds like they want both of us. Let's get moving."

Though Leonard had to slow down as he and Nancy passed through each bulkhead, he virtually flew down the corridor, swinging his leg to get as much speed and momentum from the crutches as possible. Just as his arms began to burn from the exercise, they arrived at the command deck. Commander Krylov was seated in a chair in the center of the room studying a sheet of paper while the rest of the crew worked dutifully at their stations. The atmosphere on the command deck was different than it had been over the last few days; more electric and alive. Nancy and Leonard could sense anticipation building in the crew for some unknown event.

"Commander Krylov? Some of your crew came to the medical ward and said you wanted to see us?"

Krylov straightened in his chair and swiveled around at the sound of Nancy's voice. "Ms. Sims. Mr. McComb? What on earth are you doing out of bed?" Krylov rose and hurried to Leonard's side, helping Nancy ease the injured man into a nearby seat.

"Thanks for that." Leonard said hoarsely. Out of breath from their mad dash to the command deck, he gasped loudly for a moment, feeling the blood pound through his heart and injured leg. Krylov started to call the doctor over, but Leonard refused, holding his hand up and shaking his head. "No, I'm fine. What did you want to see us about?"

Krylov kept a nervous eye on Leonard as he addressed the pair, somewhat worried about whether Leonard might collapse to the floor. "I'm terribly sorry that the request for your presence was delivered in such an apparently urgent manner. I just wanted to show Ms. Sims some new satellite imagery we obtained so that she and you could give us your opinions of it, Mr. McComb."

Krylov picked up a laptop and held it out for Nancy, who took it and sat down next to Leonard. The two of them looked at the satellite imagery on the screen, unsure of what they were seeing at first. "What are we looking at?"

"This is imagery from forty-five minutes ago at the canal, where we'll be crossing in a day or so. Zoom in on the lower half, and tell me what you see clustered on and around the bridge."

Leonard tapped a few keys and the image changed, magnifying the location Krylov specified. A bridge was visible, stretching high over the canal. Four lanes wide, it was not empty or filled with vehicles, as Leonard and Nancy were expecting, but instead it was filled with bodies. Thousands of creatures packed together as they streamed across the bridge. Creatures were spread out across every square inch of visible land on both ends of the bridge, and from a series of images taken a few moments apart, it was clear that they were moving rapidly northward as they disregarded every obstacle in their path.

Rachel Walsh | Marcus Warden | David Landry
11:17 AM, April 24, 2038

"One… two… three… lift!"

Rachel, Marcus and David all grunted as they strained to lift the thick steel track on top of one of the wooden ties that had been laid down in the gravel. With Rachel at one end of the beam and Marcus and David at the other, they worked to slide and push the track onto the edge of the tie before stopping. Frequent breaks had been a requisite part of their work considering that each of them was still dealing with the injuries they had sustained, but the work was moving along smoothly, though not as quickly as they had hoped.

"Nice job guys… let's get this one hammered in." Rachel smiled at David and Marcus who were leaning against each other, groaning from the efforts of their exertion. Each of them only had the full use of one of their arms, so they fell in naturally to helping one another, working to support and brace each other as they moved the heavy equipment on the tracks. Hefting a long-handled hammer into the air, Rachel motioned toward a pile of spikes on the gravel. "Who wants their fingers pinched?"

With a grimace, Marcus leaned down and held one of the spikes vertically over a hole in the rail flush with the wooden tie, keeping it at arm's length and turning his head away. With a flourish, Rachel raised the hammer above her head and brought it down on the spike. Splintering the wood as it traveled forward, the spike dug a full inch into the wooden tie before stopping. Marcus pulled his hand away and stood up as Rachel brought the hammer down again, delivering several more blows to the spike before finally stopping. She let the head of the hammer fall to the gravel near her feet and drew her arm across her forehead, looking at the dark cloud cover above.

"Just a few more to go, and we'll be ready to test it out." As each length of replacement track was pulled on to the ties, Rachel continued to attach the two together with railroad spikes. Compared to a professional job, the work was sloppy and sub-par, but it was enough that even David's attitude began to improve.

The normal passage of time marked by the sun was non-existent thanks to the storms, and by the time Marcus glanced at his watch, it was nearly midnight.

He, Rachel and David were all exhausted as they walked the length of the track, pointing out the small and large flaws and strengths in the work they had performed. While the replacement rail wouldn't hold up to repetitive travel, the three agreed that, if their luck held, it might just allow the locomotives and a few of the train cars to pass before giving way under the stress.

Marcus and David collapsed on the ground near the locomotive. Their heads hung to their chests and sweat dripped from their faces, falling to the dirt with the tiniest of splashes. Rachel stood over them for a moment as she surveyed the rail before she sat down next to them, taking a proffered bottle of water from Marcus. The three sat quietly for nearly an hour as they rested, watching Sam wander around the newly constructed rail as he sniffed what seemed to be every piece of gravel and every inch of wood, iron and steel. Finally, after they had recovered a bit from the day's work, Rachel pushed herself up to a standing position and looked back at the train just behind them.

"What do you say, guys? Can we get the cars uncoupled and test this out tonight?"

Marcus's first instinct was to laugh, lie down, and go to sleep. With a sigh, though, he took Rachel's outstretched hand and stood up next to her, helping David up along the way. The three stood together for a moment, looking at the makeshift railroad and the massive train that they were hoping the rail would somehow support.

"Well," David said as he walked toward the locomotive, "time to find out whether we're going to fail or not."

The couplings holding the train cars together were simple to unlock and, together, David and Marcus unlocked the one between the third and fourth train cars, leaving the locomotives and three boxcars connected in the lead group. As they worked on the coupling, Rachel pored over the controls in the lead locomotive, trying to learn them well enough to start the lead engine up. Without warning, the locomotive engines came to life, causing David and Marcus to jump away from the train. They ran to the lead locomotive which had already started inching forward, pulling themselves in through a side door.

"Were you going to warn us about that?" Marcus shouted over the sound of the engines as Rachel worked the controls frantically.

"Sorry! A little busy here! Did you uncouple the cars?"

"They're disconnected and we're ready. How far will we go, though? Just to the edge of the repaired track?"

Marcus, David and Rachel all grabbed frantically for handholds as the train lurched forward. Rachel jabbed at several buttons, but it was no use. "I think the train's in an automatic startup cycle! I don't know how to stop it!"

Unburdened by the hundreds of tons worth of boxcars it had been towing previously, the train accelerated quickly down the track, speeding toward the repaired section at a much faster pace than Rachel had planned. She had hoped to move the train slowly along the repaired area while David and Marcus walked on either side, checking to make sure the repairs would hold up under the train so that they might have a chance to fix any problems as they came up. The train had its own agenda though, and the power of the locomotives all working in unison drove them forward inexorably with no chance of stopping.

Leonard McComb | Nancy Sims
2:28 PM, April 24, 2038

As Leonard stepped through the bulkhead, Nancy kept her arm outstretched, preparing to catch him in case he tripped. While he had shown remarkable improvements over the last day, Nancy was still concerned about the fast pace Leonard was forcing upon himself after such a major operation. Refusing to listen to any of her arguments, though, Leonard insisted on being allowed to exercise vigorously, mainly by walking for hours through the vast corridors of the Arkhangelsk.

Since last seeing Commander Krylov, Nancy and Leonard had spoken little about the satellite imagery of the canal, though it was weighing heavily on both of their minds. When Leonard finally stopped to rest and eat, Nancy took the opportunity to discuss the situation with him over a bowl of suspicious-looking stew.

"How far do you figure until we're there?"

Leonard looked up at the wall clock and shrugged. "A few hours maybe. We should get an hour or two of sleep if we can beforehand. Krylov's probably going to want us up there with him while we go through the canal."

"Any ideas as to why they're all traveling north? There had to be hundreds of them."

"Tens of thousands. And that's just what we could see. I'm guessing they're heading to the same place as the ones we saw on the way west, starting at Samuel's compound."

Nancy snorted at the mention of Samuel's name and nodded thoughtfully. "Probably to the nexus, then. Same place we're headed. I don't like that one bit. Dealing with the AI's one thing, but those creatures are going to make it even worse."

Crumbs flew across the table as Leonard bit into a large cracker too aggressively. After swallowing he lowered his voice, looking around to make sure no one was listening. "Krylov seems to like you. He's listened to your opinions so far, anyway. Maybe you can convince him to deal out a bit of destruction on our way through the canal so we can slow the creatures down a bit. It might not do all that much in the grand scheme of things, but who knows."

Nancy nodded and then turned to look at a door opening at the other end of the room. Past a few crewmen who were also partaking in the meal, as if on cue, Commander Krylov stepped through the bulkhead. Looking around, he spotted Nancy and Leonard and nodded to them before taking a dish and filling it with a small portion of stew and packaged crackers. Greeting the crewmen as he went, he walked toward Nancy and Leonard and sat down next to Leonard, giving him a clap on the back as he looked at Leonard's bandaged leg.

"Mr. McComb; how goes the exercise?"

Leonard smiled and shrugged. "As well as it can, I guess. It hurts like hell, but your doctor's done a good job taking care of everything."

Krylov dug a spoon into the stew, making a face as he put it in his mouth. "He's doing a fair sight better than our cook, I'm afraid. Poor bastard drew the short straw after the landing party incidents." Krylov picked up a cracker and opened the package, pushing the stew away in the process. "As bad as it is, though, you'd both better get as much in you as you can stomach. We're coming up on the crossing in two hours, and I would appreciate your assistance up on the command deck, Ms. Sims, and yours as well, Mr. McComb, if you can manage."

Leonard slapped the thigh of his injured leg and smiled broadly. "Nothing I can't handle, Commander. We were actually just discussing the canal before you arrived."

The commander raised an eyebrow as he took a small bite from the cracker. "Oh? Please enlighten me. I could use as much information going into this as I can get."

Leonard looked at Nancy and she took a deep breath before speaking. "We haven't talked about it much, but we're in agreement that the creatures' goal is to reach the nexus. They're traveling in huge swarms like the ones we saw when we were going from Washington to Alaska."

"Any particular reason why they'd be trying to reach this 'nexus' that you can think of?"

"We were just starting to discuss that when you arrived." Leonard interjected. "It's likely that the AI is gearing up for the next step it's taking, whatever that is. You know the theories that we were throwing around, but there's no solid evidence for any of them yet."

"What we do know," Nancy said, "is that letting those creatures get to where they're going is anything but a good idea."

Krylov's eyes narrowed as he glanced back and forth between Nancy and Leonard, a slight smile gracing his face. "I have the feeling you're about to ask me to do something, yes?"

Nancy reached out and patted Krylov's arm, smiling as she did so. "Very observant, Commander. Leonard and I agree that any disruption in the creatures' movements could be beneficial. Since we're passing through the canal anyway, we were hoping that there might be some way to prevent any more of them from crossing over the canal."

Krylov looked at the surface of the table for a long moment as he quietly stroked his chin. "Hm. I think we can manage that." He stood up, tossing the uneaten half of his cracker into his lukewarm stew. "Follow me and I'll show you a few options at our disposal."

Rachel Walsh | Marcus Warden | David Landry
11:09 PM, April 24, 2038

The sound of gravel being pulverized under the wheels of the locomotive was harsh over the sound of the engines themselves. David, Marcus and Rachel all winced at the noise, but with nothing they could do about it, they held on and hoped for the best. Tucked in a corner and whining loudly, Sam cowered in fear at the sounds surrounding him. Marcus reached out a hand to comfort him, only to be thrown to the floor as the locomotive rocked from side to side. Metal ground upon metal as the wooden ties shifted under the weight of the train, causing the tracks to begin to fall out of alignment. With only a few ties placed, the amount of stress on the spikes and ties was enormous, and the entire repaired section was under threat of collapse.

"We have to stop! It's not going to hold!" David screamed in Rachel's ear, fighting to be heard.

"It's not like we have a choice anymore! Just hold on!" Rachel shouted back at David as she watched through the front of the train to see the repaired section coming to an end. "We're nearly there!"

Another lurch rocked the train in the opposite direction and the cold snap of steel chilled Marcus's spine. David and Rachel were thrown across the narrow confines of the locomotive while Marcus barely managed to maintain his hold on a nearby seat as he sank to the floor to try to get to a safer position. As he watched out the window, the black clouds ahead began to tilt crazily to the left before rocketing back to the right as the train lifted several inches up and then slammed back to the ground. Though the lead engine had gone through the repaired tracks without an issue, the stress caused by the subsequent engines and boxcars was too much for the meager assortment of wooden ties and spikes. The rails began to break off from the ties, sending the spikes rocketing through the air due to the sheer amount of pressure they were under and widening the width of the rails to the point where the rear cars were no longer in full contact with them. No longer constrained by the rails, the rear cars began to wobble, causing the entire train to pitch back and forth and setting up a resonance that threatened to derail the entire set of cars.

Frantically pawing through the controls, Rachel tried desperately to find something to slow the train down, but as she pushed and pulled on a series of buttons, switches and small levers, one of them caused the train to jolt forward even faster. The engines went into overdrive as the throttle was pushed to its maximum and the train struggled to find traction to pull the rear boxcars through the last few feet of the now nearly re-destroyed section of repaired track. Although this increase in speed wasn't the result Rachel had hoped for, it was the one that ultimately resulted in success. Instead of stopping and hoping that the oscillation of the train would cease before the locomotives and boxcars were thrown off the tracks, the increase in speed broke the resonant frequency set up by the fishtailing boxcars, causing them to straighten out as the back and forth motions of the train ceased. A final horrendous squeal of metal upon metal signaled the end of the repaired section of the track as the boxcars' wheels locked back into the rails with several satisfying thumps. Free of the abrupt panic brought on by the near-disastrous experience, Rachel remembered the emergency lever she had used previously to stop the train and placed her hand on it, preparing to pull it downward.

Marcus's hand came down on Rachel's and pulled it off of the lever as he pushed her to the side. "No! We're clear! If we stop again, we'll have to go through all that startup nonsense again!"

Hearing Marcus's voice cleared the clouds in Rachel's mind and she stepped back and sank to the floor, her back against the wall of the locomotive. Instead of the sound of scraping metal or spikes being torn from wooden ties, the only sounds were the engines of the locomotives and the clicking of train wheels on the tracks as it continued to pick up speed. The steadily increasing clicks were oddly soothing to Rachel, who found herself timing her breathing to them as she calmed down and tried to recover. Sam poked his head out from his hiding place and crawled up to Rachel, nuzzling his head in her lap and whining softly as he looked for comfort from their ordeal.

"I hope we didn't forget anything because we're definitely not going back that way." David was leaning halfway out of a window as he looked back at the formerly repaired section of track that was now in ruins. The wooden ties were askew, with one of them having sunk far enough into the gravel that the rails connected to it had physically broken under the weight of the train as it passed over, making it impossible for anything to cross over the area again. Marcus and Rachel instinctively looked around them, verifying that they had indeed loaded all of their supplies onto the train, and thankful once again that nothing of importance had been lost in the APC's explosion.

Leonard McComb | Nancy Sims
6:36 PM, April 24, 2038

"So, what do you think?" Commander Krylov strode down the center of the brightly lit chamber, lifting his arms and gesturing to either side. The immense room filled the forward portion of the Arkhangelsk, running from the bottom to the top of the ship and extending out to both sides. Rows of large cylinders stood upright to the left and right of Nancy and Leonard as they followed Krylov, gazing around in awe. Radiation symbols were affixed to the tubes, along with long and cryptic metal signs filled with Cyrillic script. One third of the tubes were several feet in diameter while the rest were of smaller sizes all the way down to just two feet. As Krylov continued to lead them forward, Leonard noticed that the orientation and styling of the cylinders changed abruptly. Instead of being nearly featureless and standing upright, the tubes at the front of the chamber were laid out horizontally in large stacks along the outer walls.

"Torpedo tubes, I assume?" Leonard nodded in the direction of the horizontal tubes and Krylov stopped to see what Leonard was referring to.

"Ah, yes. Indeed. For both forward and aft launching. Good against targets in the water, though I'm afraid they won't do much to the creatures on the surface."

"What about the nukes?"

"I think you're forgetting something." Nancy spoke from behind Leonard as she peeked through a small window in the side of one of the torpedo tubes, examining the weapon inside. "The nanobots feed off radiation. We'll destroy the creatures, but feed them at the same time."

"Damn… how could I forget that?" Leonard muttered, putting his hand to his forehead.

"Nancy is correct, Mr. McComb. From my study of the data you provided, if it comes down to us being responsible for destroying the nano-robots and their nexus, we'll have one shot at destroying enough of them to cripple them before they can start rebuilding themselves. We can only use the nuclear devices on the nexus if we hope to maintain the element of surprise."

44

Leonard leaned up against one of the torpedo tubes, taking his weight off his good leg and the crutches. "Well I would assume you've got *something* non-nuclear that you can use out of the water. Right?"

Krylov's blank stare and his hesitation at responding to Leonard's question gave Nancy and Leonard the only answer they needed.

"Well shit, Krylov. How're you fixed for spit?"

A puzzled look passed over Krylov's face before he ignored the colloquialism and continued speaking. "Unfortunately, Mr. McComb, you are correct; our only surface-to-surface weapons are nuclear, as was our loadout when we left port." Walking to a set of locked containers in a corner, Krylov extracted a key from his pocket and opened one of them, pulling out a large gray object and holding it aloft. "We do, however, have this."

Krylov threw the object toward Leonard, who caught it and turned it in his hands, examining the writing. Warnings were emblazoned in not only Russian, but in six other languages, including English. "WARNING: HIGH EXPLOSIVES! HANDLE WITH CAUTION!"

Leonard looked up at Krylov, a thin smile crossing his face. "Nicely done. How're we going to plant it without getting overrun by the creatures, though?"

"That, Mr. McComb, will be simple. If you're ready, please follow me again."

Krylov walked back down through the chamber the way they came, leaving Nancy and Leonard standing alone. Leonard threw the explosive back in the crate where Krylov had retrieved it before pulling his crutches back under his arms. Nancy walked next to him as they hurried to catch up to Krylov, who was already at the doorway leading into the room.

"I think you offended him." Nancy whispered in Leonard's ear.

"He'll get over it. Besides, he could do to be stirred up a bit when we get there."

The walk to the next attraction was shorter than the first. A brief walk up a flight of stairs led them to a dimly lit area near the top of the submarine, an area that seemed oddly familiar to both Nancy and Leonard. Krylov stopped near a flight of stairs that went upwards into a closed hatch, then he pointed at the floor.

"I believe you left something of yours here, Mr. McComb."

The dark metal of the stairs and floor around them was discolored. As Nancy's and Leonard's eyes adjusted to the lighting, they both realized why the stairwell felt familiar.

"You're going to send your men up on deck to place the explosives by hand?" The disbelief was plain to hear in Leonard's voice as he ignored Krylov's poor joke about the dried blood that still coated the stairs. Nancy started to respond to Krylov's remark, not liking the tone in which he made it, but Leonard stopped her, shaking his head slightly as he didn't want to make any sort of fuss about it.

"Of course, Mr. McComb. The canal's width is such that the men should be able to plant explosives at both sides of the bridge with ease before we submerge to go underneath. If they work quickly and quietly enough, I assume they should be able to do it without drawing the creatures' attention, yes?"

"I... guess it's possible." Leonard was starting to second-guess the idea of trying to destroy the bridge, wondering if it was worth the risk, when Krylov clapped his hands together and smiled broadly.

"Well then, it's settled." He glanced at his watch, raising an eyebrow as he looked back at Leonard and Nancy. "You'd both be wise to get some rest. We'll be arriving shortly, and I'll need you close by when we do. I'll send a crewman to retrieve you then."

Krylov turned and walked quickly away, leaving Nancy and Leonard to stand alone together in the dimly lit hallway.

"Is it just me," Nancy said, "or does Krylov seem a bit off compared to when we first met him?"

Leonard replied cryptically as he watched Krylov disappear around a turn. "Things aren't always as they seem."

Nancy sighed and turned around, trying to remember how to get back. A sign nearby with a small red cross on it had an arrow pointing in the opposite direction from where Krylov had gone. They followed the arrow dutifully, slowly making their way back to the medical ward.

Rachel Walsh | Marcus Warden | David Landry
11:52 PM, April 24, 2038

"Hell yes!" Marcus's outburst was accompanied by a short jump and a quick pump of his arm in the air. Stretching his arm out, he grabbed Rachel and David, pulling them in tightly for a hug. Overcome with a sudden feeling of happiness and excitement, Marcus's smile was contagious, and Rachel and David quickly found themselves joining in with the impromptu celebration.

"I still can't believe that worked!" David craned his head out the window again. Though they had traveled too far to still be able to see the damaged section of track, he was still marveling over the fact that their repairs had held up long enough to allow them to get by.

Marcus slapped David on the back and grinned from ear to ear. "Have some faith in us, David! Pulling off the impossible is what we're meant to do."

"Apparently so." Rachel sat slowly down on the floor and smiled, shaking her head in disbelief. The tension caused by the long ordeal had finally broken, snapping like a rubber band and leaving her overcome with a sense of relief. Despite the fact that they were still nowhere near where they needed to be, they had—against all odds—managed to both recover from Doe's attack and deal a retaliatory blow that had taken him out of the picture. This realization led to another, more sobering one that quickly erased her smile. Noticing her sudden change in mood, Marcus and David sat down next to her.

"What's up?" Marcus asked playfully, still smiling. "Wish we had left him alive or something?"

"Of course not." Rachel's glare was subtle, but behind it stretched more rage and fire than Marcus had seen before, instantly making him regret the joke. "But with him out of the way, all we've got left is the AI to contend with."

"Sorry, but isn't that a good thing?" David broke in, looking at Rachel in confusion.

"Oh, sure. It's great. But compared to fighting the AI, dealing with that megalomaniac almost sounds like a walk in the park. It wasn't, but... well, you know what I mean."

48

Still confused, David stood up and dug into his bag, pulling out a dust-covered bag of chips. "Better one than two," he said, stuffing a handful of chips in his mouth. "Besides, we've got a trump card with Bertha. When we reach the nexus, all we'll have to do is fire her up and the nanobots should be gone just like that."

"I hope you're right." Rachel sighed heavily and stood up, stretching her arms and legs as she rose.

"Okay, that's enough doom and gloom for now." Marcus jumped to his feet. "We'll have plenty of time for that later. For now, we need to set up a watch pattern. I'm feeling alert enough, so I'll go first. David, you can go next, then Rachel."

Standing there at the front of the locomotive, one arm bound in a sling with bandages taped across his shoulder, Marcus looked like he had been to hell and back. His attitude, on the other hand, was that of a boisterous three year old once again, happy and full of energy. Rachel smiled at him, glad to see that he was beginning to return to his old self. After being worried about him, and how he and David were behaving toward each other, it was good to see a positive change in the midst of everything that was going on.

As Rachel stretched out near the back of the locomotive with Sam curled up next to her, she couldn't help but think about Marcus's question. *"Wish we had left him alive or something?"* Having the thought of Doe to deal with had kept her marginally distracted from the larger picture. With that distraction now gone and left by the side of the tracks to rot, she had no other choice but to face the AI head on, including the numerous implications that came with it. Doing so meant dredging up thoughts and feelings she hadn't considered for many days. Rachel closed her eyes, but instead of darkness, the image of her daughter flashed by, followed by her husband and her home. Cities that she had passed through, the remnants of bodies, burned out cars and collapsed buildings all came trickling back to the forefront of her thoughts, though they didn't come alone. A slow, steady buildup of guilt accompanied them, along with a profound sense of emptiness. A rustle from David several feet in front of her suddenly made her wonder. *Does he feel the same thing?* If David felt a similar measure of guilt for what had happened, he didn't show it.

Mike Kraus

Leonard McComb | Nancy Sims
7:02 AM, April 25, 2038

The clear skies that had allowed the Arkhangelsk to obtain imagery of the canal persisted through the morning. Commander Krylov rotated the periscope slowly as the Arkhangelsk sailed the last few miles down the coast past Veracruz on its way into the first section of the canal. The soft tap of rubber on the metal floor made Krylov turn around and he smiled as Nancy and Leonard approached him.

"Ms. Sims! Mr. McComb! So good of you to be here." There was no trace of the dark sarcastic humor Krylov had shown earlier in the darkened hallway. Nancy and Leonard had gotten no sleep, having spent the last few hours discussing Krylov's strategy to take out the bridge the creatures were using to cross over the canal.

"Commander." Leonard nodded and sat down in a seat next to the periscope. Krylov stepped back and motioned for Nancy to step forward.

"Please, take a look, Ms. Sims. Place your arms on the handles and use them to turn left and right."

Nancy pressed her forehead against the padded surface above the eyepiece, well-worn from years of use. The bright light of the rising sun made her squint as her eyes struggled to adjust. As the outside world came into focus, Nancy began to see the coastline take shape, with beaches, trees and a few scattered houses near a large runway in the distance. As Nancy slowly rotated the periscope, her hand brushed against a button on the side of one of the handles, causing the magnification of the scope to change. Everything in her view suddenly leapt forward, appearing larger than it had before and startling her in the process.

To someone who hadn't spent weeks traveling cross-country and witnessing destruction on a scale never before seen by mankind, the few shattered buildings and scorched fields in the distance might have appeared to be the result of a fire or an earthquake. Nancy knew differently, though, recognizing the tell-tale patterns of destruction that told of bombs that had fallen close by.

"Commander Krylov?" Nancy stepped away from the periscope, rubbing her eyes. "It looks like at least one nuke was dropped nearby. Are you sure the canal's clear?"

Krylov pointed at a nearby computer screen and nodded. "Everything we looked at indicated that it was. The area was hit hard, but the canal was out of the danger zone for most of the damage from what we can tell."

Nancy looked at Leonard who nodded slowly. "Let's hope you're right, Commander."

Leonard jumped in next before Krylov had a chance to reply. "Mr. Krylov," he said, deliberately avoiding the use of Krylov's position as a test of sorts, "the Panama Canal isn't exactly short. The imagery we saw was only of a fraction of it; aren't there other bridges that run across?"

If Krylov was bothered by Leonard's use of the term "Mr" instead of "Commander," he didn't show it. "Oh, but of course, Mr. McComb." Krylov motioned to the same computer screen again as he pushed a few keys, pulling up a wider satellite view of the area they were entering. "There are three main bridges through the area. One at the start, one near the middle, at the automated locks, then another near the end. These bridges appear to operate as both pedestrian, train and vehicular ones, which makes our job much easier."

Leonard whistled softly as he stood up, leaning forward on his crutches to examine the image up close. "That's a lot of concrete and steel to take out without getting spotted. Are you sure we can do it?"

Krylov nodded. "We don't have a choice, Mr. McComb. Unless you can think of another option."

Leonard shook his head and sat back down, idly rubbing around the stump of his leg. "Not really another option so much as wondering how we'll pull it off, especially in broad daylight when these things'll be streaming across the bridges like cockroaches during spring cleaning."

Commander Krylov pointed at the screen again, tapping the locations of the first and last bridges. "From the last pass of scans we were able to obtain, it looks like these two bridges get the least amount of traffic. Most of the creatures seem to be congregated around the central one. For the first and last bridges, we shouldn't have any trouble getting the explosives set. For the middle one, though, you may be right. But it's a risk that you and Ms. Sims made clear that we need to take to try to delay these things as long as possible.

"Once all sets of explosives have been set and we're clear of the final bridge, we'll blow them all at once to ensure that we're nowhere near when it happens. It's an imperfect plan to be sure, though I see no other option."

"All right," Nancy said, looking to Leonard for his silent confirmation, "how long until the first explosives are planted?"

Krylov looked at his watch. "We have approximately fifteen minutes until we reach the first bridge when we'll surface and plant the first set of explosives."

"Mind if we go up and watch?" Leonard stood up and balanced on his crutches, demonstrating that while he might have been knocked down, he was anything but out. "We'll stay out of their way. Plus, we might be of some use."

Krylov hesitated, nearly denying Leonard's request before relenting. "Very well. Don't leave the stairwell, though. If we have to close the hatch in a hurry, you two cannot be anywhere close to it."

Leonard turned and started hurrying toward the exit, calling over his shoulder as he departed with Nancy. "No problem!"

Ten minutes later, Leonard and Nancy stood near four men in the blood-stained stairwell. The men looked nervous, more with themselves and the task they were about to perform than with the two strangers standing nearby. Nancy kept her arm around Leonard to help him balance as they waited for the hatch to open.

"How much longer?" Nancy whispered to Leonard, who shrugged in response. A soft flashing amber light answered Nancy's question, as did a loud mechanical rumble from the direction of the top of the wide stairwell.

Light burst through cracks in the hatch as it rolled open, flooding the compartment with fresh air, the smell of the ocean and the sound of rushing water. The Arkhangelsk had barely surfaced as it was passing under the first bridge on its way to the locks as the helmsman fought to balance stealth and speed. The depth of the canal was less of a worry, since there was more than enough room for the Arkhangelsk to remain fully submerged and make its way through.

Radios strapped to the crewmen's chests crackled and a terse order was issued. They immediately ran up the stairs, exiting onto the exterior of the Arkhangelsk. Two of the men ran for the port side while the other two headed to the edge of the starboard. They dropped to their knees as a shudder ran through the ship, causing Leonard to tip forward, nearly losing his balance. The ship came to a near stop and began to surface faster, bringing them high on the water.

When the submarine finally finished moving, the men extracted sets of tubes from bags carried on their backs and began aiming them at the bridge supports high above their heads. Small black shapes flew from the tubes and landed on the steel of the bridge with rhythmic thumps as the magnetic sheaths wrapped around the plastic explosives kept both the explosives and their detonators attached to the bridge. Even as high as the Arkhangelsk was in the water, launching the explosives at the high points of the bridge was risky, and more than one failed to attach because it simply didn't gain enough altitude. The combination rail, vehicular and pedestrian bridges were all of the bascule drawbridge variety, designed specifically to ensure that ships of all heights passing through the canal could get through. A high arch on the first drawbridge meant that the explosives couldn't be evenly distributed, but instead had to be clustered around both ends.

The total time the four crewmen took to affix the explosives to the drawbridge was under two minutes, after which they hurried back down the stairwell as thousands of creatures continued to stream over the structure high overhead. One of them spoke softly into his radio and the hatch began to close as the submarine sank back into the water, moving forward to the next target.

Rachel Walsh | Marcus Warden | David Landry
5:07 AM, April 25, 2038

"Rachel!" Marcus's voice was low, but he still managed to hiss at her as he spoke, communicating a frightening level of urgency and panic. "Wake up! We've got problems!"

Rolling over and pushing herself to her knees, Rachel crawled forward, joining Marcus and David who were each crouched behind a control panel, peeking above it to watch out the side of the train. Sam lifted his head to look at Rachel and she shook her head at him, whispering for him to stay still.

"What's going on, guys?" Rachel slid in between David and Marcus, who both pointed through the window. After meandering through the woods for a while, the tracks converged with a highway, running parallel to it for several miles. Out on the highway, illuminated both by the glimmer of the rising sun and lighting from the storms, Rachel saw the reason why David and Marcus were both staying hidden. No more than fifty feet away, thousands of creatures were moving together down the road heading south. Changed individuals both old and young made up the group that was larger than Rachel could have imagined. The creatures paid no attention to the train as it passed them by, whipping down the tracks at top speed, just as it had when it was under the control of the creatures previously.

Marcus turned around and sat down on the floor of the locomotive, taking a deep breath and exhaling slowly. "Damn… that's a *lot* of them."

"These migrations seem to be getting much more common." Rachel whispered. "I guess it's time for them to all congregate at the nexus."

Marcus peeked back up at the window, watching how quickly they were traveling compared to the creatures. "Well that's no problem. We'll get there way before the creatures do, going this speed."

"True, but who's to say that the AI's going to wait for every creature to reach the nexus before launching its next step? What about creatures in the rest of the world? I'm not sure they'd be able to make it here, let alone in any reasonable time frame."

"That…" David turned around as well, trying to think of a good reply, "that's a very good point. What about those creatures? Separated as they are from the nexus, they won't be able to get here. So what's going to happen to them?"

"Couldn't there be other places where they're building these nexuses?" Marcus's question was met with a quick shake of David's head.

"Definitely not. I would have seen them on the satellite scans. Whatever they're doing, they decided on this particular location, luckily for us. I'd hate to be stuck trying to get across the Atlantic."

"So what happens to these things when the nexus is gone?" Marcus looked at Rachel, repeating David's question.

"Your guesses are as good as mine. They might self-destruct, try to re-form in swarms or who knows what else. It doesn't really matter, though. Not now, anyway. We just have to destroy the AI before it does whatever next-level bullshit it's trying to do. We can worry about mopping up the survivors afterward."

The answer Rachel gave was unsatisfying to the three of them, but with nothing better it was the only one they had. Getting back on their knees, the group resumed their watch of the creatures, occasionally pointing out a particularly disfigured or odd looking one as they tried to make light of the admittedly frightening situation. Though the creatures had no idea that Rachel, Marcus and David were on the train, if they found out they could easily derail the train and ensure that the three wouldn't make it to the coast.

The tracks continued along next to the road for several more minutes before branching away, back into the woods and fields as it had before. With the creatures long out of sight, the trio all breathed a collective sigh of relief and sat back down on the floor of the locomotive. Too filled with adrenaline, Rachel and David had no more interest in sleeping and instead busied themselves with organizing their supplies. David started to set up his computer and electronics that he had taken from the APC before it was destroyed while Marcus and Rachel took stock of their food and water and examined the controls of the train in detail.

Marcus glanced over at David sitting on the floor, hunched over his computer as he was examining satellite imagery. "Hey David, where do you think we are?"

"Hm?" David turned and looked at Marcus, distracted by what he was looking at.

"Our location? Any ideas?"

"Oh, sorry. These aren't live images; there's too much cloud cover for that." David sighed and closed his eyes, rubbing his temple as he tried to figure out where they were. "Somewhere in the Carolinas, I'd guess. I'm not exactly sure where this particular track goes, though."

Rachel leaned over David's shoulder, taking a look at his computer. "That's something we need to figure out soon. If this train was on its way to the gulf as we assumed, there could be a track changeover that we need to take to get there."

David nodded. "Two steps ahead of you there. I'm looking through some of this older imagery to try and figure out what track we're on, then I should be able to tell you exactly how we'll get there."

Marcus leaned back against the wall, looking out at the sharp shadows cast from the trees by the flashing lightning. "I wonder how Leonard and Nancy are getting on. It'd be nice to at least know that they're alive."

There was no response from either Rachel or David as they all thought about Leonard, Nancy and the submarine, hoping that—somehow—a miracle was being pulled out of a hat. The only sounds in the locomotive for several minutes were the engine, Sam's gentle snoring, and the tap of David's fingers on his laptop keys. Locked in a battle with the computer, he worked tirelessly until, finally, he spoke.

"What the hell..."

Rachel looked over at him lazily, then caught sight of what was on the screen. "Hey! You connected with the satellite!"

David nodded slowly as he stared at the screen, a curious expression on his face. "Yes, just temporarily. It's down again, but... this can't be right.

"The satellite log shows that there was a login from... the Pacific Ocean. Not too long ago, either." He looked up at Rachel and Marcus, turning the screen more so that Rachel could see the data herself.

"How on earth can you know that someone in the Pacific was looking at the satellite?" Marcus raised his eyebrow as he asked the question.

"GPS coordinates. The satellite records the location of every access attempt for security, plus a whole host of other information, too."

"If I had to guess," Rachel said, interrupting David as a smile slowly built on her face, "then I'd say that Leonard and Nancy are not only alive, but on their way to us as we speak." She jabbed her finger at the screen, pointing to a collection of letters that Marcus didn't recognize. "That's not one of our machines, and it's certainly not anything I've seen from a US government computer."

Rachel's smile was infectious, and Marcus and David quickly found themselves grinning along with her, overjoyed at the knowledge that Leonard and Nancy were most likely alive, well, and bringing some much needed backup to the fight.

Leonard McComb | Nancy Sims
11:39 AM, April 25, 2038

In the haze of smoke and confusion, Leonard wasn't quite sure where things had gone wrong. Thirty seconds earlier, he had been standing at the bottom of the stairwell next to Nancy, watching as the four crewmen launched explosives onto the second bridge while another two crewmen ascended a ladder on the wall of the lock, climbing toward a nearby control room. Thousands of creatures were pouring across the bridge above the Arkhangelsk, but despite the massive size of the vessel and the noise made by the crewmen on her deck, the creatures on the bridge were paying them no mind. Out of nowhere, though, several events unfolded at once that radically changed the situation.

The roar of one of the creatures cut quite clearly through the sound of them walking and running across the bridge, which in turn caused hundreds of the creatures surrounding it to stop walking and look for the source of what had made it cry out. One of the four crewmen on the bridge, frightened by the creatures overhead, prematurely detonated the explosives with an emergency detonator, causing a chain reaction with the rest of the explosives. However, since an uneven amount of explosives had been placed, it did not collapse with the precision that Krylov had planned to happen when they had long since passed the locks.

Twisted shards of metal both large and small filled the air, churning with huge plumes of smoke and flames. Bits of the bridge began to rain down onto the Arkhangelsk and Nancy pulled Leonard back, nearly toppling him over as they ran several feet down the corridor to escape from the debris crashing in through the open hatch. Hundreds of the creatures on the bridge were killed instantly at both ends where the explosives were laid, and the survivors howled in rage, focusing their attention on the destruction to find its cause.

Of the four crewmen on deck when the explosions went off, three were killed almost immediately by pieces of the bridge swinging and falling downward, scraping along the hull of the Arkhangelsk as they went. The fourth was able to dive through the hatch, barely escaping a massive piece of the bridge that hung in the air, swinging back and forth before finally crashing down, sending a shudder through the entire vessel. Alarm klaxons began to howl throughout the ship and Krylov shouted into the radio, trying to figure out what had happened.

With the bridge in tatters—and much of those tatters now on top of and in the water around and below the submarine—there was still the matter of passing through the locks to deal with. The filling and draining sequences were fully automated, yet they required someone in the control room in a tower overlooking the central bridge to start them up. The two crewmen assigned to this task were very nearly shaken off of the ladder leading up the side of the lock to the control room, but they managed to hang on through the turmoil.

Looking back, they were both in shock at seeing the carnage below them. In addition to the bridge having been half destroyed and the creatures injured and enraged, their escape route back through the Arkhangelsk's hatch was now cut off by the massive pieces of steel that lay twisted on the deck, blocking all entry and exit. Creatures were leaping from the bridge onto the submarine's deck far below, some of them falling still as they broke limbs while others managed to stay intact and began tearing at the debris that covered the open hatch.

"Move!" The crewman lowest on the ladder shouted at his companion, who was staring at the mayhem with his mouth hanging open. Startled, he looked down and then up before resuming his climb. With another thirty feet to go before reaching the control room, both men hurried as quickly as they could until they reached a metal hatch. The lead man pushed against it with his shoulder and it popped open with a clang. Both men pulled themselves into the control room, the lead man going straight for the controls with a radio in his hand while the other pulled a submachine gun from a bag strapped to his back before taking up a guard position near the main door to the control room.

On the Arkhangelsk, the situation had gone from bad to worse. The sound of creatures landing on the hull above them spurred Leonard and Nancy to race down the corridor, limited only by the speed at which Leonard could throw himself forward with his crutches. The creatures tore at the metal debris covering the open hatch, effortlessly removing enough of it in the space of a minute to allow themselves easy entry down the stairwell and into the submarine itself. Letting Leonard get ahead of her to jump through a bulkhead doorway, Nancy turned and saw a dozen creatures racing toward her, the red alarm lights reflecting in their silver eye sockets.

"Move your ass!" Leonard reached out for Nancy, tugging her roughly through the doorway before raising his hand and firing several shots from a pistol that had somehow materialized there. Nancy held her hands over her ears as the sounds echoed off the corridor walls, making every shot sound like a miniature explosion. Three creatures fell to the floor in the corridor before Leonard pushed against the open hatch door, swinging it shut to block the creatures from continuing through. Seeing Leonard struggle, Nancy crawled forward and pushed as well, giving the door enough of a shove to close just before the creatures slammed into it. Leonard quickly twisted the wheel on the door, locking it tightly before he jammed one of his crutches into it, keeping the creatures from unlocking it.

"We need to get moving to the command deck before those things get there." Leonard moved his remaining crutch to the right side and balanced on it while motioning from Nancy to move to his left. He placed his left arm around her shoulder for support and started hopping forward, moving as quickly as he could. Behind them, the creatures shattered the thick glass on the door, howling madly as they threw themselves against it, trying to no avail to break through. After they had turned a corner and closed another hatch, Leonard stopped and sank to the floor, pulling a handheld radio from his pocket and thumbing the button.

"Krylov, this is McComb. The creatures are on board. You need to seal up as many hatches as you can and get us the hell underwater, *now!*"

On the command deck, Commander Krylov's face turned white as Leonard's voice came over the speakers. Turning to his dive officer, he shouted, resisting the urge to knock the man from his chair and perform the operation himself. "Dive, damn it! Dive! Get us as low as possible!"

He then turned to the rest of the skeleton crew, desperately wishing that he wasn't running out of men so quickly. "Arm yourselves and begin to seal the bulkheads leading to the surface exits. If you see anything not human, shoot it!" The men he was addressing scrambled to obey, running through multiple exits from the command deck to obtain weapons and proceed through the ship.

Back in the control room overlooking the lock, the lead crewman looked over the controls, quickly finding the one required to begin the filling process. Connected to diesel generators below ground and solar panels strung along both sides of the lock, the control room and the lock itself was still fully operational, and needed only the touch of a single button to operate.

"Commander, we're in position!"

Static filled the radio for several seconds, then Krylov's voice came through, barely audible over the sound of alarms in the background. "Start it now! Hurry!"

Below them, the massive vessel began to sink into the water. Air bubbles rose to the surface from the open hatch, churning the water and disorienting the creatures around the ship as they continued to try and make their way in. The two men in the control room watched the ship sink for a few seconds as they resigned themselves to their fate before activating the console and starting the automated filling process that would allow the Arkhangelsk to pass through the locks.

Nancy and Leonard had stopped to catch their breath again. Lost in some section of the ship that Nancy didn't recognize from her earlier explorations, she was doing her best to get them to the command deck, but had so far been unsuccessful. Gunfire and distant voices—both human and not—had echoed through the corridors, making them uncertain as to the current situation involving the creatures.

"Leonard?"

Leonard was sitting on the corridor floor opposite Nancy, thumbing the radio button to no avail. He looked up at her, breathing heavily from his exertion, wincing at the stabs of pain that would occasionally lance through his leg.

"What?"

"Where did you get that?" Nancy pointed at the radio. "And the gun, too. Where did you get them?"

Leonard smiled as he massaged his knee. "Krylov needs to pay a bit more attention when he lets strangers into his weapons rooms. I snagged the gun and the radio on our way out, just in case we needed them at some point." A loud clang echoed through the corridor, sounding closer than any of the other noises had been. "I wish I would have grabbed more than one pistol, though..."

Leonard pushed himself up with Nancy's help and they continued on their way, moving as quickly and as quietly as they could. Since sitting down and getting back up again, the noise level had gone down, and there was only an occasional burst of gunfire followed by a howl or scream. All of the wall signs were marked in Russian with arrows pointing in various directions and no clear indication of where the command deck was. As they continued to move forward, though, the sound of gunfire gradually grew louder to the point where the sporadic bursts were coming from behind a doorway in the next corridor down. Leonard and Nancy stopped and leaned against the wall, trying to decide if they would be safer retreating or hoping that whoever was shooting wasn't being overwhelmed by the creatures.

Leonard McComb | Nancy Sims
12:28 PM, April 25, 2038

"Keep it up! They're nearly all dead!"

Commander Krylov was kneeling behind his chair, looking down the sights of a rifle that he kept pointed at the one door that was left open to the command deck. Behind him, the rest of what remained of the Arkhangelsk's crew stood in various positions, all brandishing weapons ranging from Makarovs to AK-74s. Every few seconds, a creature would dart past the open door, testing the crew's defenses and reactions, trying to gain entry to the room and kill the last of the people on board.

A shot rang out from behind Krylov, who shouted at the man without bothering to turn his head. "Do not engage unless you have a sure shot!" Ammunition was beginning to run low, and Krylov wasn't certain how many creatures were left on board. In the moments since the bridge had collapsed over the Arkhangelsk, Krylov had been shocked at how many creatures had gained entry to the submarine as well as how quickly they had swept through the ship, trying to kill anyone who stood in their way. His men had performed bravely, manually closing off hatches and activating emergency bulkhead seals that prevented the Arkhangelsk from completely flooding, though the vessel's response was sluggish due to the amount of water she had taken on. More of the flooded areas would have been sealed off if not for the creatures, though, which nearly overwhelmed the small crew.

Quickly honing in on the retreating crew, the creatures had congregated around the command deck, which Krylov had the foresight to seal off, leaving one entrance intentionally open to try and keep the creatures busy with so that they wouldn't go on a rampage through the rest of the ship. Seven creatures had died to hails of gunfire and one of the crew on the command deck had been injured so far after he got too close to one of the beasts that hadn't been properly finished off.

Another creature ran past the open door, hooking its hand around the frame and swinging in, staying low to the ground to avoid being shot. Krylov tracked the creature with his rifle and fired several short bursts, sending all but two rounds directly into the creature's side and chest. It collapsed to the floor, sliding several inches before coming to rest in front of a petrified crewman who it had been trying to reach, adding another body to the seven already lying just inside the door to the command deck.

Behind Krylov, the groan of a hatch lock being disengaged made him turn. A figure was visible through the small window in the door, though he couldn't make out if it was human or one of the disfigured creatures. Another burst of gunfire came from one of the crewmen and a howl came from the corridor as another creature darted by slowly enough to take a few bullets in the side. The hatch on the opposite side of the room began to open and Krylov tightened his grip on his rifle as he prepared for an assault by the creatures from two directions.

"Don't shoot!" Nancy stepped through the door with Leonard right behind her, leaning on her for support as he hopped over the threshold and began to pull the door closed behind him. Krylov lowered his rifle and looked at Nancy and Leonard with a stunned expression, shocked that they had survived long enough to make it to the command deck.

"Leonard! Nancy!" Krylov's formal way of addressing the two had disappeared as his accent had grown stronger from the stress he was under. He glanced at Leonard's hand and belt where he carried the empty pistol and the radio that he had taken from the equipment locker. Looking back at Leonard for a long moment, he weighed the option of giving the man another weapon.

"Can you shoot?" Krylov picked up a rifle from the floor and threw it at Leonard who caught it with one hand. He dropped down on his one knee and swung the upper half of his other leg around, sitting on a step near the back of the room with the rifle placed firmly against his shoulder.

"I can manage."

Krylov nodded, relieved, then looked at Nancy. She held out her hands expectantly and Krylov threw her a rifle as well, raising an eyebrow in surprise. She caught his look and shrugged as she slid the bolt back and chambered a round. "Women don't shoot in your country, Commander?"

The oddity of Nancy's statement caught Krylov off guard and he laughed involuntarily as he turned around and resumed his watch on the door. Try as he might, he couldn't stop himself from laughing, and was soon joined by Nancy, Leonard and a few nearby crewmen who had heard what she said as well. The laughter spreading on the command deck in the midst of the battle was infectious, and Krylov soon found himself wiping tears from his eyes as he struggled to keep focused on the open door.

When the last of the creatures assaulted the room, throwing themselves through the open door in a desperate attempt to kill the people inside, they were not met with fear but with laughter, focusing the attention of each person with a laser-like precision. The attention was accompanied by a hailstorm of bullets that tore through metal and flesh alike, destroying the creatures' attempt in a few short seconds. The juxtaposition of conflicting emotions sat strongly with Leonard in particular, who was the first one to stand up and make his way toward the creatures' bodies, hobbling along on his crutch.

Krylov stood up and joined Leonard, then Nancy, who took Leonard's arm and placed it on her shoulder. The three stood with the crew behind them, staring at the mangled bodies of the creatures on the floor as their laughter gradually died out. Krylov cleared his throat and turned to his crew, smiling grimly at them.

"I think that's the last of them. Get us a head count started, then get us moving again. Once we're clear of this damned canal we'll surface and take stock of the damage."

The crew moved slowly at first, stepping gingerly over the creatures strewn across the floor until Krylov yelled, clearing the last of the happy mood from the air. "Get your asses moving *now!*"

Everyone, including Leonard and Nancy, jumped at Krylov's order, and the crew broke into sprints, hurrying to their stations and down the hall to find missing crew and prepare to get the submarine moving again. Leonard held out his rifle to Krylov who looked at it and shook his head, pushing it away. "Keep it, Mr. McComb. We might need it again."

Leonard and Nancy looked at each other and began moving toward a pair of vacant chairs. Krylov spoke again, raising his voice so that the crew left on the command deck could hear him. "Excellent work, by the way. Not just you two. Everyone. Now let's get out of here, shall we?"

Andrey Lipov | Sergei Usov
Panama Canal Main Lock Control Room
12:42 PM, April 25, 2038

"If we get back to that ship, I'm never getting off again."

Andrey snorted at Sergei's comment as they watched the dark form of the Arkhangelsk move slowly forward through the open gates of the lock. The ship was submerged, but they could still see it as it passed through the water, clearing the lock gate and escaping the carnage that had surrounded it.

After the unexpected destruction of the bridge, Andrey and Sergei had watched nervously as the lock filled with water, hoping that no critical systems had been damaged by the explosions. Though the process took several minutes to complete, it eventually finished, and the lock's water level was equalized with the river ahead of the ship. Andrey and Sergei had heard of the complete redesign of the canal (like most of the world), though they had never seen it in person. Neither had they imagined that the process of operating the single lock system would be so easy, making the multiple locks used previously look complicated compared to the current process.

Instead of refitting and reworking the existing locks, canal, and artificial lake, the new system actually involved a completely separate canal placed just a quarter of a mile from the old one. The twisting path of the old canal was discarded for a direct one, drawing a straight line through the land. Surprisingly, this was more cost-effective than attempting to enlarge and modernize the old canal, which is what most people had assumed would happen before the final engineering plans were made public.

Automated in ways that the old canal was not, the new construction consisted of two massive locks, each capable of holding supertankers whose size dwarfed that of the Arkhangelsk. In between the locks was a canal wide enough for ten of the supertankers to fit side by side, a distance calculated to be both cost effective and most efficient given a study of the current ocean traffic at the time and planning at least seventy-five years into the future.

The two locks were closer to the center of the canal than the ends, and once a ship or group of ships entered one, the control room operator would activate the lock by simply pressing a single button. The lock would close, fill with water to equalize the height with that of the interior canal, then it would open, allowing the vessels inside it to proceed through the canal. At the same time, the lock at the opposite end was closed and equalized as well, through a completely automatic process that required no operator assistance. Because of the timing of the opening and closing of the locks, vessels larger than individual or family-sized craft had to register their passage at least two hours in advance to be guaranteed a slot on the schedule. If, for some reason, a vessel encountered engine or other troubles while traversing the distance between the locks, there was enough room for it to remain for some time for repairs without it interfering with the passage of other ships.

Though the project was initially seen as a vast waste of resources, the benefits it provided were recognized within the first three months of its service. Supertankers previously relegated to sailing around the southern tip of South America were able to pass through the canal for the first time, shaving weeks off of their travel schedules and enabling more goods to be transported across the world faster than was possible with the old canal.

"So what now?" Andrey was looking down the ladder at the canal where they had come from, shaking his head. The only other exit from the control room was a winding staircase out the other side which ended near the road leading to the bridge that, until a short time ago, had been swarming with creatures. Peeking out the door leading to the staircase, Andrey could see that there were still creatures milling around the edge of the bridge, staring at their compatriots on the southern side of the canal who could no longer go north from their current location.

Sergei stood and watched the creatures with Andrey, his finger rubbing nervously on the trigger guard of his rifle. "We wait them out. What other choice do we have?"

Andrey's shoulders slumped and he rested his head against the wall of the control room, sweat pouring down his face and neck. "Then I guess we won't make it back, will we?"

The older of the two cousins, Sergei looked at Andrey in pity, wishing that he could somehow save them. Going through their equipment inventory in his mind, his eyes started to dart back and forth as the seed of an idea began to blossom. He pulled his pack off of his back and knelt down in front of it, rifling through the contents until he found what he was looking for. Sergei pulled a set of three grenades out and held them up for Andrey, who took them, holding them at arm's length.

"What are you thinking?"

Sergei ignored Andrey's question and pulled out his radio, tuning it to the frequency that the Arkhangelsk was listening on and depressed the microphone button. "Arkhangelsk, this is Usov. Come in, Commander." A burst of static came back and Sergei quickly turned the speaker volume down. Andrey glanced down the staircase to see if the creatures had heard the noise, but if they did, they showed no signs of caring one way or the other.

"Arkhangelsk, come in!" Sergei hissed, trying to keep his voice low and the panic from rising in his throat. "Respond, damn it!"

Another burst of static was cut off, replaced by the sound of a hand fumbling with a microphone before a voice came through. "Krylov here. How the hell are you still alive, Usov?"

Sergei grinned and responded, his eyes locked with Andrey's as he spoke. "Commander, Lipov and myself both made it. We're stuck in the control room, but we may have a way out. Do you have a way to get us back on board if we can make it to the second lock?"

"*Shit.*" Krylov thought quickly estimating how much time it would take for them to reach the second lock, and how much he could spare before they had to pass through it and place explosives on the third bridge. Doing so meant that they would have to open the second hatch to the deck of the submarine, assuming the port section wasn't flooded like the starboard, and that they didn't have any more unwelcome guests on board to contend with.

Shit, shit, shit! Krylov had the presence of mind to keep further repetitions of the word to himself as he juggled the logistics in his mind, finally coming to a decision.

"You have thirty minutes to get yourselves in the water past the second lock's far gates. After that, we have to get to the last bridge and then get the hell to open water to assess our damage."

Andrey and Sergei's faces both paled as they looked out the window of the control room, seeing the second lock far in the distance. Even without having to deal with the creatures, running from the first lock to the second would scarcely be possible, though as their only choice left, they had no other options.

"We'll be there. Usov out."

Andrey Lipov | Sergei Usov
1259 PM, April 25, 2038

"Keep your head down and go. Hurry!" Sergei whispered at his younger cousin, urging Andrey to get down the stairwell as quickly as possible. After speaking with Commander Krylov on the Arkhangelsk, the pair had waited in the control room for a few moments, watching as the creatures below started to disperse. At the slow rate at which they were going, it was going to be hours before they were fully gone, though, and Sergei and Andrey didn't have the luxury of waiting around for that length of time.

Rifles at the ready, Andrey and Sergei descended the stairs rapidly, cringing with each footstep that echoed off of the aluminum structure. The creatures on the ground still seemed uninterested in the pair so they continued moving quickly until they reached a gate at the end of the stairs. Closed with a padlock and a loose chain, it was quickly opened with a pair of bolt cutters pulled from Sergei's pack, and Andrey swung it open slowly, keeping his gun trained on a collection of creatures wandering north, away from them.

The gate at the bottom of the stairs exited onto a narrow path next to the road that went over the bridge that used to extend over the canal. Separated from the road by a flimsy chain-link fence, there was nowhere to hide from the creatures along the walkway for a good hundred feet, where it split from the road and dropped down into a maintenance passage that went along the thick wall on the edge of the canal.

So far, so good, Sergei thought, tapping Andrey's shoulder and pointing towards the maintenance passage. Hidden from view as it was, it was the only certain way to move quickly along the canal without being spotted by the creatures. Moving slowly and deliberately, the pair quickly reached the passage unnoticed by the nearby creatures, who were still milling about, completely unconcerned by their surroundings.

Not accustomed to dealing with the creatures, Andrey and Sergei began to relax, feeling cautiously optimistic about their easy escape from the control room. As they made their way along the maintenance passage jogging in the same direction as the Arkhangelsk, Andrey began to hum to himself, quietly at first, then louder as he felt more confident about their safety. This continued for less than a minute before he stopped, panicked, turning to look at Sergei as the screams of multiple creatures came from just above them, at the edge of the canal wall. The sound of breaking branches and running feet joined the screams, causing Sergei's eyes to widen as he pushed his cousin forward, the two of them breaking into a full-on run.

From behind them, three creatures dropped into the passage. Two landed on their feet and began immediately running after Sergei and Andrey while the third miscalculated its jump, toppling over the edge of the canal wall into the water below. Twisting his upper body as he ran, Sergei fired off a short burst from his rifle, sending plumes of concrete dust spraying into the air. The lead creature howled in pain and was quickly overtaken by its comrade who ignored the pain, focused intently on the two men ahead. The sound of the gunfire did little to aid Sergei and Andrey's stealthy escape, and they heard the distant sound of several more creatures crying out.

The maintenance passageway was filled with crates and low-hanging pipes and fixtures, forcing Sergei and Andrey to duck and squeeze their way around obstacles to keep from getting their clothing or equipment hung up. The creature had little difficulty, choosing to tear obstacles out of the way rather than dodge them. Seeing that there was no way to outrun their pursuer, Sergei opted for a somewhat less nuanced approach that he hoped would both take care of the immediate threat and slow down subsequent ones. Reaching into a pouch on his vest, Sergei pulled out a small block of explosives encased in the same high-powered magnetic material used to attach explosives to the bridges. While the explosive in Sergei's hand wasn't as large as those used on the bridge, it still packed a powerful punch, and would be more than enough for what he was planning.

With so many exposed metal surfaces in the service passage, it was easy for Sergei to locate one to attach the explosive to. Ahead of them by a good fifty feet, a large metal plate was leaning against the outer edge of the maintenance passage that caught Sergei's eye. "Andrey! Move faster!" He held the explosive up to eye level as Andrey swung his head around. Upon seeing the small block in Sergei's hand, Andrey's eyed widened and his speed increased as a jolt of adrenaline surged through his body. By the time they reached the metal plate, they were several feet further ahead of the creature than before. Sergei quickly looked behind him, judging how far they were from the creature before he threw the explosive at the plate, satisfied by the solid *thunk* of it attaching to the thick steel.

Out of the same vest pouch that he had retrieved the explosive, Sergei drew a small detonator and thumbed a safety switch on the side. A light on the detonator glowed red and he glanced back, watching the creature quickly close in on the explosive. Just before the creature reached it, Sergei jammed his thumb down on the detonator's button, causing the red light to turn green. In the same instant, the temperature of the maintenance passage increased dramatically and a thunderous sound and shock wave rocketed through the air, nearly toppling Sergei and Andrey off of their feet.

Concrete and steel exploded outward, showering the water below with pieces of all sizes. The creature chasing after Sergei and Andrey was annihilated in an instant as the maintenance passage began to collapse around the damaged area, blocking off any idea of retreat back the way they came. The deafening noise was audible from miles away, attracting multiple groups of creatures who descended upon the newly formed hole in the canal wall like vultures. Not pausing or slowing down, Sergei and Andrey continued running, putting as much distance between themselves and the creatures behind them as they could.

With the aid of the well-timed distraction, Sergei and Andrey were unmolested by creatures for the remainder of their run, a fact they appreciated wholeheartedly when they fell against a gate at the end of the passage, exhausted. A lock on the gate was quickly broken and they moved forward cautiously, struggling to control their labored breathing as they exited the maintenance passage and returned to the surface.

A second control room that was a mirror image of the first one—though this one had no bridge nearby—was in front of them, and below it stretched a ladder all the way down to the water's surface. Access to the ladder was available only through the control room, which meant climbing a tall staircase before opening a trapdoor and descending down the ladder. There were no creatures in the immediate area as Sergei and Andrey climbed up the ladder, taking the stairs three at a time. Sergei glanced at his watch, cursing silently. *One minute. Shit!* Thumbing the radio transmitter, Sergei spoke quietly into it, hoping any creatures that might be nearby wouldn't hear them.

"Arkhangelsk! We're here! Where the hell are you?"

As if on cue, a great dark shape rose from the waters of the lock directly below the control room as the submarine slowly rose to the surface. Pieces of the bridge still clung to her hull and the starboard hatch was still open and jammed full of debris. As the deck cleared the surface, the port hatch began to open, revealing two men who stood at the top of the stairwell, looking up at the control room. Sergei and Andrey fumbled with the trapdoor over the ladder for a few seconds before throwing it open with a clang and beginning their descent. With the sub fully inside the lock, the automatic equalization process began and the water began draining from around the Arkhangelsk. After a few tense, nervous moments of descending Andrey and Sergei jumped from the lower rungs of the ladder, landing and rolling to a stop on the sub's deck. The two crewmen waiting for them helped them to their feet and the four quickly disappeared inside the sub, the hatch closing immediately after them.

Once safely back inside the ship, the two men fell to the floor, throwing their bags and weapons to the side as they gasped for air, eagerly accepting canteens of water held out for them by someone who stepped out from the shadows. "Excellent work." Commander Krylov stood before them, smiling as they took the canteens from his hands and began drinking noisily from them. "Our guests didn't think you would make it. I'm very glad to see you proved them wrong."

Without another word, Krylov turned back down the hall, leaving the four men standing alone to stare at one another. After a few moments, when Sergei and Andrey had caught their breath, the elder cousin looked at the two men who had helped them into the sub. "What about the last bridge?" The man smiled and held out his hand, helping Sergei to his feet while his comrade did the same for Andrey.

"Come up and we'll see the fireworks together."

The Arkhangelsk kept on course out of the canal for a full mile before stopping. Commander Krylov had the feed from the periscope routed through several monitors on the command deck so that everyone could watch when the explosives on the final bridge went off. The fireball was small, but visible, and the crew confirmed that the explosives on both the first and last bridges had detonated successfully. An event that should have brought cheers only brought a few sad smiles and a host of determined faces. After opening all of the deck hatches, Krylov ordered the few remaining crew to take stock of the damage and clear the remaining debris from the ship. In the medical ward, Leonard slumbered as Nancy sat nearby, keeping watch over him as they waited for the Arkhangelsk to start the final leg of the journey.

Rachel Walsh | Marcus Warden | David Landry
3:35 PM, April 27, 2038

The midday sun was warm overhead, a surprising and welcome change from the storms that had been plaguing the eastern seaboard for days. A soft wind blew gently through the overgrown grass, reminding Rachel of the summers spent at her grandmother's home in Texas. Closing her eyes, she could imagine herself back there now, lying on her stomach in the tall grasses as she watched insects climb over each other, consumed in their small world and completely unconcerned with anything outside of themselves. The dream broke apart, fragmenting as she opened her eyes again, staring in disbelief at the massive structure that stretched in front of her, dwarfing everything around it.

The tower was a mixture of dark gray and black, a roughly rectangular shape, albeit with various odd angles built in at unexpected places. There were no windows visible, though the unusual shape created the illusion of various crevices and cracks in the exterior of the structure. It was impossible to tell whether the crevices led to anywhere inside the tower, but they added a great deal to its intimidating appearance. With a wide base that gradually tapered off into a narrow top, the bottom of the tower was easily a mile on each side. Staring at the tower for more than a moment or two at a time made each of the trio's stomach's uneasy to the point where they had to look away or close their eyes lest they grow more nauseous.

Though the structure was still a few miles away, the sheer size of it was unsettling to Rachel, David and Marcus. Living in New York, Marcus was used to seeing large buildings, but the scale of the one in front of him made his mind spin as he tried to comprehend the sheer magnitude of it. Lying on the other side of Rachel, David was slack-jawed. The size of the structure on the satellite images had appeared large, but in person it was breathtaking and puzzling to say the least. Standing near a wide bend in a river, a portion of the base of the structure was actually in the water while the rest of it was spread out over an area that appeared to be a combination of fields and demolished buildings.

"What the hell do these things need with a skyscraper?" Marcus's question was a whisper. No one said anything for a moment afterward, as they all continued to take in the enormity of what lay before them.

"Looks like it's almost finished." Rachel pointed to the top of the structure. "I can't imagine they can build much higher, given how the width is shrinking so rapidly as it goes up. It's got to be a kilometer and a half tall already." Rachel pushed back from the edge of the small hill they were lying on and stood up, stooping over as she walked the few feet back to the train. After seeing the structure in the distance, they had figured out how to slow the train down to a crawl until they found a vantage point that partially sheltered them from view of the tower. Although they doubted that they would be noticed so far away, none of them were about to take any chances when they were so close to reaching the end of their journey.

"C'mon, let's not waste any time." Rachel waved for David and Marcus to follow her. They all hurried back to the train, hopping inside and closing the door behind them. Sam whined softly from his spot at the back of the locomotive, tucked into a small nook between two control panels. Rachel patted his head as she got the train moving again, taking care to increase the throttle speed manually instead of triggering the automatic startup process they had used after repairing the track. As the train started moving forward, David and Marcus went around to each of the small windows and ensured that they were both closed and that their sheer blinds were pulled down and secured. The blinds weren't good for much else than cutting down on the sunlight, but being as close as they were to the nexus, none of them wanted to take a chance and be spotted by the creatures.

As David started powering on his computer equipment and Rachel kept a close eye on their speed, Marcus kept watch out the front of the locomotive. The track they were on looked new, and as they continued forward, signs of construction became more and more common. The trees, fields and hills gave way to flat, burned land, with only the stumps of trees and ashes of vegetation remaining. The sunlight began to fade from the sky, and the group initially thought that a storm was rolling in, though the truth was somewhat more disturbing. As the single railroad track began to branch into two, then four, then eight, then sixteen, then a seemingly endless number, the shadow from the tower ahead of them stretched across the fields, blotting out the sun.

Rachel felt her stomach grow sick as she thought back to her first sight of the nanobot swarm just after waking in the basement where her home once stood. The circle was nearly complete as the end approached, reaching up to the sky like a spear that threatened to pierce the very heavens themselves. Though the nexus and the AI that was very nearly finished constructing it was formidable, Rachel's hopes of success hadn't wavered thanks to the unassuming object that sat quietly in the boxcar, awaiting its activation. This comforting thought vanished when David's panicked whisper echoed through the locomotive, nearly causing time itself to stop as Marcus and Rachel looked at each other, an expression of horror on their faces.

"Bertha's not responding!"

Leonard McComb | Nancy Sims
3:39 PM, April 27, 2038

Standing on the deck of the Arkhangelsk, Commander Krylov looked up to the tall fin, shielding his eyes from the sun with a thickly gloved hand. The sudden sound of metal scraping on metal caught his attention and he turned back just in time to jump out of the way of a ten-foot section of a bridge support slipping off the side of the Arkhangelsk and plunging into the water. The two men who had been pushing on the support looked at him awkwardly as he shook his head and began to help push the next piece off.

The work to clear the Arkhangelsk's deck was slow, primarily due to the low number of crew available to work. Having to split them between clearing the hatch and deck and pump water out of the flooded compartments didn't help matters, but both tasks were necessary if they wanted to continue forward. In addition to jamming open the starboard stairwell hatch, the pieces of the bridge that became lodged on the deck of the submarine were also jamming two of the missile hatches. The water, thankfully, didn't seem to have affected any important systems, but it would be a few more hours before enough of it was drained for the crew to start investigating the damage caused by it. In the meantime, the crew below deck worked pumps to clear one compartment at a time while the crew on deck continued to cut and push sections of the bridge into the water.

Though Leonard had wanted to help in some capacity, Nancy refused to let him, going so far as to take his crutches away so that he had to remain in bed and rest. Spotted bleeding combined with an overall paleness and exhausted look made Nancy nervous, and she had insisted that he spend the day resting, especially considering the situation they would be going into once the ship was repaired. After receiving a grumbled promise to remain in bed from Leonard, Nancy headed to the command deck where Andrey, the younger of the two cousins who had activated the canal locks, was sitting, keeping an eye on the ship's systems. Sitting down at a station next to him, Nancy smiled and took a deep breath, looking at the controls spread out in front of her, all marked with symbols that were foreign to her.

"So... is there anything I can help with here?"

"Your country created these things, yes?" Andrey's question was not one of accusation, but curiosity. Ignoring her question, he didn't look at her as he spoke, keeping his eyes trained on the screens in front of him instead.

Nancy was somewhat taken aback at his question, and couldn't think of an appropriate response for a moment. Andrey looked over at her, watching her struggle to come up with an answer before finally settling on the simplest one she knew. "Yes. As far as I know. I mean, who knows if we had help from others, but from everything I know, yes. We created them."

"I see." Andrey pushed a few buttons, changing the display on his monitors and jotted a few notes down on a pad of paper. When he was done, he looked at Nancy again. "Why?"

Nancy snorted and laughed, amused by Andrey's pointed questions. "Who do I look like, the President?" Andrey looked her up and down and shook his head, making Nancy laugh again. She sighed deeply and pondered his question, trying to come up with an adequate answer.

"I don't know. Power, probably. Control. The usual set of reasons."

"But it killed your country. It killed everyone. What kind of power is that?"

Nancy thought about Mr. Doe, remembering the things Rachel had shared about the enigmatic man. "It didn't kill everyone. Besides, I don't think these things were ever meant to do this. The people who made them lost control of them, and they had no way of stopping them."

Andrey nodded slowly and pushed another set of buttons. Graphs and numbers flashed across the screen and he wrote down a few more notes before looking at Nancy again.

"If the people who made this could not stop it, how can we?"

To that question, Nancy didn't have an answer at first, until she remembered her conversations with Leonard about how much she had changed in such a short amount of time.

"If I can survive a nuclear holocaust, find my way across the country, meet up with a group of strangers and somehow manage to make my way *back* across the country, all while avoiding being killed by a radical cultist, then somehow find a Russian submarine off the coast of Alaska, I'm pretty sure this submarine can handle those things." Nancy smiled as Andrey tried to process what she had just said. "Besides, we're not the only ones out for blood. I doubt we'll even be needed, what with Rachel and Marcus there."

A crackle came from speakers on the command deck, and Krylov's voice followed. "Attention all crew and guests. The surface of the ship has been cleared. Mr. Lipov, please get us underway at one-half power, maintain depth. We'll continue to clear flooded compartments as we go. Once they're empty, we'll be able to submerge and return to full power again."

Andrey jumped out of his seat and hurried to a different station while Nancy swiveled in her seat, watching him go. A few control manipulations later and Nancy felt the surge of power in the submarine as the engines engaged, propelling the mighty vessel forward in the water. As Andrey monitored their speed, he noticed Nancy watching him and pointed to the seat he had been occupying. "You want to help?" Nancy nodded eagerly and slid over into the next chair as Andrey continued. "Good. Observe the screen. When levels go over one hundred, write down time with pencil. Understand?"

Nancy looked down at the clipboard in front of her, then at the screen. Cyrillic characters raced by along with numbers at the top, with an ever-changing graph below them that had markings on it ranging from zero to one hundred and twenty-five. While she didn't understand what she was looking at, Nancy picked up the pencil and stared at the graph, jotting down the time displayed on the wall clock each time the graph surged past the one hundred mark. Andrey nodded approvingly, his shoulders relaxing as he continued to focus on their speed, monitoring it closely along with half of the other systems on the ship.

Rachel Walsh | Marcus Warden | David Landry
3:56 PM, April 27, 2038

"David, if this is a joke, I will not hesitate to kick your ass up one side and down the other."

David's pale expression was not a reassuring response to Rachel's forced attempt at humor. "Shit!" she mumbled, leaving the controls and hurrying to his side. "What's wrong with it?"

"I can get a connection established, but that's it. The systems won't respond at all. I can't activate it or power it on. Nothing works!" David jumped to his feet, slamming his laptop shut and throwing it in his bag as he ran for the back of the locomotive. "I'm going to check directly; yell if you see something bad coming!"

Rachel reached for David, trying to stop him, but he slipped past her and threw open the door at the back of the lead locomotive. A short hop and a quick climb around to a side door was all that was required to enter the next locomotive, and he did so easily, going down the train quickly and without any signs of danger. A slight squeal from the wheels and a jerking motion evidenced Rachel's liberal application of the brakes, though she was cautious to not put them on too hard lest they attract attention. Attention from what, though, none of them was certain, as all of the tracks and land surrounding the nexus tower were devoid of activity.

As David opened the back door of the last locomotive and started to step forward, he clung to the door and jerked his foot back in, his face pale as he realized that there wasn't just a step and a door access into the boxcar ahead of him. Instead, a ladder was mounted on the front of the boxcar, and below it was the coupling device, rails and bare ground. David cinched the bag up on his back and kept one arm inside the locomotive, holding on while he reached out with the other to grab on to the ladder. His fingers brushed a rung and he relaxed his other arm, falling forward and grabbing the ladder at the same time. Butterflies soared in his stomach for the instant that he was falling forward, but the ladder held firm and he started to climb, reaching the top in just a few seconds.

David guessed the train was traveling at roughly twenty miles an hour, but any speed other than a full stop was nauseating from his position on the top of the train. With no other way to enter the boxcar than through a vent in the top,

David pulled himself up from the ladder, rejecting the idea of standing or crouching on the top in favor of crawling on his stomach. Keeping his arms and legs spread in an attempt to keep from sliding off, David shuffled his way forward, finally reaching the vent. Sitting an inch above the top surface of the boxcar, the vent was easy to pry off, though as soon as the front portion was lifting, it caught the wind and blew away, bouncing loudly on the next few boxcars before landing with a loud clatter on the rails behind the train. David winced with each sound, hoping that there was nothing nearby to hear it. The hole in the roof of the boxcar was barely large enough for someone to squeeze through, so David unfastened his bag and dropped it through before turning around and sticking his feet in. He pushed himself backwards through the vent, grunting as his waist, chest and then finally shoulders slid through.

Instead of dropping directly to the floor of the train like he had anticipated, David's feet hit the cold metallic surface of Bertha, just next to where his bag was sitting. He hopped off and pulled his laptop back out of his bag and turned it on, hoping that the close proximity to the device would solve the problems he had been facing in the locomotive. As he tapped key after key, scrolling through screens and changing every setting he could think of, his heartbeat became harder and more rapid. Nothing was working or changing, despite his best efforts; Bertha was still unresponsive.

Rubbing his hand across his mouth as he took a step back from the computer, David looked up at the open vent, wondering if he could get back out the way he had come in. With nothing else left to do, David climbed up on top of Bertha and jumped for the vent, bracing his hands along the edges and pulling himself upward and back onto the roof of the boxcar. Moments later, he burst in through the back door of the lead locomotive, sweat pouring down his face and neck as he gasped for breath. Rachel hurried to his side as he sat on the floor, shaking his head and muttering to himself incoherently. Rachel shook his shoulders and hissed at him, struggling not to yell. "What happened? Did you fix it?"

David looked up at Rachel, his eyes filled with a mixture of defeat and exhaustion. "I can't get the damned thing to activate. The explosion when Doe destroyed the APC must have damaged her somehow, internally."

Rachel sat down next to David, staring at the floor. "Shit. That's it, then."

"You two really going to give up that easy?" Marcus stood over Rachel and

David, looking down at them like a father lecturing a pair of misbehaving children. "If so, we should probably radio the sub and let them know we don't need them anymore."

"How are we going to contact the submarine, Marcus?" Rachel looked up at him. "There's no way to tell where they are, and if we just start transmitting blindly, we'll attract the attention of whatever's holed up in that tower."

Marcus squatted down and looked Rachel square in the eye. "You're probably right. And when that happens, we'll deal with them just like we've dealt with them every other time. We'll kick their asses."

Marcus stood up and held out his hands, one for Rachel and one for David, waiting to see what they would do. Rachel looked at David and shook her head at him. "You sure Bertha's down?"

David nodded slowly. "More sure than I've ever been of anything."

"So much for the easy way out, eh?" Rachel sighed and took Marcus's proffered hand, then David did the same. They stood to their feet and looked around the locomotive's interior, mulling over what they were about to do. Marcus chuckled at Rachel's remark and hefted his backpack onto his shoulders and secured it before patting his leg and calling Sam out from his hiding place.

"Last time I checked, the only easy way out of this entire excursion is the dying part, so I think I'll stick to the hard way for just a bit longer."

Leonard McComb | Nancy Sims
4:08 PM, April 27, 2038

"Open the hatch."

Krylov unconsciously tightened his grip on his rifle as he spoke the order. Standing in a dark hallway with two others next to him, Krylov kept the rifle pointed at the floor, waiting for his subordinate to unlock the thick steel door in front of them. As the lock disengaged with a bang, Krylov raised his rifle and shouldered past the man, planting a boot at the base of the door and pushing it open. The room beyond was pitch black save for a few red waterproof lights that had survived the torrent of seawater. Flashing on and off in a slow, rhythmic pattern, the lights cast uneven shadows from the piles of equipment strewn across the room from the force of the water that had come rushing in. Krylov thumbed a switch on his rifle's flashlight, illuminating the room as he checked each corner and behind each piece of equipment, watching the water flow out through the open door.

Though the Arkhangelsk had been under way for some time, the process of draining and clearing each of the flooded compartments was progressing slower than Krylov would have preferred. As they moved deeper into the compartments, opening each door one by one and moving in the heavy hoses that pulled the water up and out, a nervous feeling in the back of Krylov's head grew more bothersome. The two men with him grunted as they struggled to move a heavy hose into position, finally letting it splash down in the center of the room, where the floor gently sloped inward. One of them spoke a few words into a radio and the hose shuddered as the pump connected to it was activated. Krylov relaxed as the water drained away, glad that they were finally reaching compartments that had only been partially flooded instead of ones that were full to the ceiling with water.

"Next." Krylov backed out of the room and advanced down the hall to the next compartment in line, looking through the glass window in a vain attempt to see what was on the other side. With a sigh, he gestured for his crewmen to take up the same positions as before, and once again he tightened his grip on his rifle as the door was unlocked. As Krylov lifted his foot to kick the door open, though, the thick steel moved on its own, jerking inward faster than any of the three men would have expected. Water poured out over their feet, distracting them just long enough to not notice a shadow move across the entrance and leap out, pushing past them as it fell on the wet floors in its attempt to escape. The creature's blurred motion startled Krylov, who spun, pulling his rifle up to aim at the beast as it thrashed, trying to gain its footing.

For a brief moment before he pulled the trigger, Krylov paused to look over the creature, marveling at it in both disgust and fear. Its body was riddled with metal and its clothes were torn nearly completely off, revealing the gaunt form of a young woman in her late twenties. Half of her hair had fallen out and her eyes were nothing more than shallow silver holes. The creature hissed and screamed at the three men standing nearby, frustrated by its inability to retreat or fight against the threat it perceived in the cold wood and metal that was pointed at its face. As inhuman and savage as the creature was, Krylov could still see the humanity that had once stood in its place.

Commander Krylov's moment of pity came to an abrupt end as the creature finally found its balance, pushing itself off of the wall and floor to run towards them. Fire roared from his rifle, deafening him and his crew in the narrow passageway as the bullets tore into the creature, shredding its head and chest and causing it to collapse limply to the floor, face down in the ankle-deep water. The entire encounter with the creature from start to finish hadn't taken more than a few seconds, and Krylov immediately turned back toward the open doorway, probing the dark interior with his flashlight in case there were more creatures inside. The presence of one of them inside a flooded chamber was alarming, especially since they had several more to clear. Once he was satisfied, he turned to his men and ordered them to continue the pumping process while he stepped back into the hall and spoke into his radio.

"Command deck, this is Krylov."

"Commander? Is that you? This is Nancy."

Krylov raised an eyebrow in mild surprise and spoke in English next. "Ms. Sims, please pass this message along to anyone on the command deck and have them contact the rest of the crew. We just encountered another creature inside one of the flooded and sealed compartments. Anyone who is working below deck must be with at least one other person, and all crew members must be armed at all times. That goes for yourself as well, Ms. Sims. Do you understand?"

"Absolutely."

"Very good. Pass this message along and ensure that you have adequate ammunition for yourself and Mr. McComb. We'll be finished draining these compartments in the next few hours and then we should be able to get underway at full speed."

Nancy's reply went unheard by Krylov as he focused his attention back on the remaining compartments. Each of the rooms that they cleared led them closer to the missile and weapons room, which had fortunately been untouched thanks to the crew's quick response. The potential proximity of the mutated creatures to the delicate and lethal devices in the missile room made Krylov nervous, and he wanted to get the area cleared as quickly as possible. He looked at the two men standing nearby who were working with the pump hose, though still casting worried glances at the dead creature.

"I'm moving forward. Follow behind as quickly as you can."

Rachel Walsh | Marcus Warden | David Landry
4:12 PM, April 27, 2038

"Is it ready?" Rachel leaned over to look at David, who was on his back, fiddling with wires under the radio panel inside the lead locomotive. He nodded instinctively, then groaned in pain as his head smacked against a metal support in the tight space.

"As ready as it'll get."

Rachel took a deep breath and leaned in to the microphone on the panel. She hesitated for a moment before finally depressing the transmit button, speaking slowly and clearly. "This is Rachel Walsh attempting to contact the Russian submarine carrying Leonard McComb and Nancy Sims. Please respond."

Rachel stared at the speaker above the console as the sound of static echoed forth from it. Three more times she repeated the message, until Marcus's demeanor changed from casually looking out the windows of the locomotive to one of tension.

"Rachel, David, get over here. Hurry!" Marcus kept his voice low, though the panic was audible even at a whisper. David pushed himself out from underneath the radio console and hurried over next to Marcus, joining him and Rachel at one of the side windows. In the distance, coming around from one of the corners of the base of the tower was a group of creatures, numbering at least a dozen, though it was hard to make out individual forms at such a long distance.

"Shit!" Rachel turned and hurried to gather up her things, dumping them in her bag before double-checking that the magazine in her rifle was loaded. "This is going to get messy *very* quickly."

Marcus put his hand on the rifle, pushing it downward as he shook his head. "There's too many of them for that right now. But I think we can use this to our advantage." He pointed at the closest section of the tower base. "There's an opening there, where one of the tracks goes. If we can keep the muties distracted and away from there, we can probably get inside."

"Inside." David's expression was one of shock. "You want to go *inside* that thing? You *are* mental! We just need to get the Russians on the horn and get a missile in the air to take it down while we run like hell!"

Marcus gestured around. "And what happens if it's electromagnetically shielded? By the time a second missile's in the air, that thing'll have plenty of time to defend itself. We have one shot at this. Assuming the Russians can actually get a missile in the air, we have to know how to take those little bastards down. Now, unless you've got blueprints for the thing stashed away somewhere, the only way we're going to be able to find any of this out is to inspect it directly, up close and personal. I'm not taking any chances with this shit, and neither should you, not when we're *this* close to winning."

The moment of silence from Rachel and David was enough to tell Marcus that he was right, and that both Rachel and David knew it.

Rachel shook her head. "We'll be screwed, though. We need to keep trying to contact the sub. If we leave the train, we won't have any radio capabilities."

David shook his head as he gathered a few tools from under the radio console and put them in his bag. "If I had known you'd be getting me into this, I would have never let you in the lab." David sighed. "I'll stay here while you two get in there and see what's going on inside the tower. The other locomotives should have radio transmitters as well, so I'll set up some kind of signal loop to keep rebroadcasting, then disconnect each of the locomotives and send them down the track ahead of us. That'll keep those things distracted while you two get in and out, then we'll retreat in the last engine back the way we came. Okay?"

Marcus shook his head, moving to block David from moving to the next train car. "Sounds good, but we're not splitting up again."

"Marcus..." Rachel placed her hand on his shoulder, but he pushed it away, stepping backwards defensively.

"Don't start with me. We are *not* splitting up."

Rachel's voice was soft, and Marcus could see the pain behind her eyes as she spoke. "We're running out of time, we need to contact the sub, and we need David's distraction to get in and out. We won't make it ten feet if we don't lure the creatures away."

Marcus's lip twitched and he closed his eyes as he rubbed the bridge of his nose with his thumb and forefinger. "Shit." He mumbled as he re-checked his backpack straps, stepping out of David's way and toward the back door of the locomotive. David nodded to him and walked past, heading for the back door before stopping, turning and addressing Rachel and Marcus together.

"I'll keep Sam here with me. Get out to the side of the second engine; you should be able to jog fast enough to keep up with it and stay out of sight from them. I'll set up a repeat broadcast in here, then push the throttle to the max and disconnect the coupler. That, plus sticking the horn in the on position should be enough to draw their attention for long enough for you to make a run for it.

"I'll keep releasing the engines one at a time to keep those things distracted. It looks like the tracks go on for quite a distance, so that should keep them away from the last one, which I'll hunker down in with Sam."

David unzipped his bag and pulled out two small devices, which he handed to Rachel and David. "Here, take these portable radios. I've been saving them for an emergency. They've got limited range and probably won't even penetrate through the tower, but..."

Rachel tucked the radio in her pocket and gave David a quick smile followed by an embrace. "Thanks, David. We'll be fine." Marcus followed Rachel's hug with a pat of David's shoulder and a grim smile, then stood by her near the door of the locomotive. David watched them with a sad smile on his face as he patted Sam's head.

David took in a deep breath and nodded at Rachel and Marcus. "Let's do it." The pair turned around and looked through the front window of the train, watching the creatures in the distance grow steadily closer. Behind them, David manipulated the train's controls for a few moments before calling Rachel to the radio. "Repeat your message; it'll be recorded and stored in the system for rebroadcasting." Rachel did as he instructed, and David waved her away to finish his work.

"Okay, it's set. In two minutes, this locomotive will go to full power and start broadcasting your message on an endless loop... I think. Honestly I have no idea if the rebroadcast will work, but we'll find out soon enough. You two need to get out and be ready to run."

Rachel nodded at David and pulled the door of the train open. It was traveling at a slow enough pace that she felt safe stepping out onto the bars mounted to locomotive, shimmying around to the side before jumping to the ground and rolling to a stop. Marcus followed her a few seconds later, then they heard the sound of David closing the door behind them. The two of them waited until the second locomotive passed them before they began to jog forward, keeping pace with the train.

Once Marcus and Rachel were out, David led Sam out the back door of the locomotive. He paused as he realized that there wasn't a way for Sam to walk easily into the next engine. Jogging along just a few feet away, Marcus noticed David's dilemma and ran up to the back of the engine, holding his hands out as he whispered at David. "Here, hurry!"

Before Rachel realized what was happening, David had picked up the large animal and tossed him to Marcus, who caught Sam and deposited him gently on the ground. David pointed toward the back of the train and shouted as quietly as he could at Marcus, trying to be heard over the sound of the train while avoiding being heard by the creatures.

"Get him to the last engine and I'll get him inside!"

Marcus patted his leg to get Sam to follow him and ran toward the back of the train while David moved towards it as well, arriving just as the lead locomotive's engine kicked into high gear and the horn started blowing incessantly. With the coupling between the first and second engines disengaged, the lead locomotive accelerated quickly, moving away from the rest of the train at a high rate of speed. As it approached the creatures, they reacted defensively, backing away from it before giving chase, running down the track in hot pursuit and ignoring the rest of the train left behind.

With the distraction in place, Marcus and Rachel had a limited amount of time to get into the tower, so Marcus scooped Sam up in his arms again, whispering softly into the dog's ear to calm him down. On his knees inside the door of the last locomotive, David took Sam in his arms as Rachel watched, relieved to see both Sam and David disappear safely inside the compartment before the door slammed shut. With David and Sam secured and the creatures momentarily distracted, Rachel and Marcus waited for the last boxcar on the train to pass by before breaking into a run, heading for the base of the tower and the entrance leading inside.

Leonard McComb | Nancy Sims
4:14 PM, April 27, 2038

"This is ***** attempting to contact ***** marine ***** rying ***** and ***** Sims. *****ease respond."

Nancy froze at the sound of a voice coming through an overhead speaker on the other side of the command deck. The voice was distorted and the message was nearly unintelligible, but upon hearing her name, Nancy raced to the radio station and grabbed Andrey's shoulder, pulling him excitedly as she spoke. "Turn it up! Quick!" Andrey manipulated the controls in front of him and the broadcast increased in volume as it repeated again.

"***** Rachel ***** contact the Rus ***** McComb and Nancy ***** respond."

Nancy turned to Andrey and spoke breathlessly. "Get Krylov on the radio!"

Working his way through the last of the flooded compartments, Krylov flinched as his radio crackled, followed by Nancy's voice once again. "Commander, this is Nancy again."

"Ms. Sims, I'm currently occupied. Please speak to—"

"*Commander.*" The tension in Nancy's voice as she interrupted Krylov caused him to stop in his tracks as he waited for her to continue. "There's a very faint radio transmission coming through from Rachel. It's repeating, and Andrey and I are trying to figure out what they're saying, but it's definitely them."

Krylov's eyes flicked back and forth as he considered what the broadcast meant. The fact that they were nearly within radio transmission range of the group on the ground meant that the time of attack, should they be forced into the situation, was growing uncomfortably close. He looked down the hall at the last three compartments that had yet to be searched and drained, then back the way he came, toward the direction of the command deck.

"Ms. Sims, I'll be on the command deck momentarily. Krylov out." With one last look at the remaining compartments, the commander turned and jogged back to where the two crewmen were still dragging the pump hose from room to room, draining the seawater out of the Arkhangelsk. He passed his rifle to the man closest to him and gave a quick explanation of what was going on, followed by a stern order. "Do not engage any creatures you see unless you're in danger of being attacked. Radio me immediately if you encounter anything unusual. Continue draining the rooms I've searched and opened, then search and finish draining the last three once you're done here. Above all, stay safe."

The two men nodded and gave Krylov quick salutes as he ran off, heading for the command deck. Once he arrived, he greeted Nancy and Andrey hastily, then stood next to Nancy over Andrey's shoulder, listening to the repeating transmission for several seconds. Behind them, the soft tapping of Leonard's crutch made Nancy turn and smile, and she ran to his side, whispering to him as she walked with him to the radio control station.

"We just started getting a transmission from Rachel. They're trying to contact us about something; hopefully it's good news!"

Leonard nodded, then addressed Krylov. "Commander, I'm not spending another second in that bed. How can I be of assistance?"

Commander Krylov looked Leonard over from top to bottom before replying. "You look better, Mr. McComb. Are you well enough to operate a radio? Mr. Lipov is needed elsewhere if you can manage it."

Leonard stepped up to Andrey's seat and waited for him to get up before plopping down in his chair with a grunt. His crutch clattered to the floor next to him and he looked up at the two Russians next to him. "Just tell me what's what here; I can't exactly read Russian very well."

Andrey gave Leonard a quick summary of the radio controls, then turned the volume on the main speaker back up so that Leonard could listen to the message a few times. Leonard turned the sound off and swiveled in his chair to address Krylov, who was standing with his arms crossed and a worried expression on his face. "Sounds like we're about to hit the shit, Krylov. Are you going to be ready with the missiles?"

"I believe so, though our current situation is less than optimal given our lack of crew. Do you have any idea when, or even if, you'll need a launch?"

Leonard tapped the controls in front of him. "That's what I aim to find out. In the meantime, though—and I don't mean to tell you how to run your boat, Commander—I strongly suggest you have those missiles ready, just in case we have to launch them."

"Stay by the radio, Mr. McComb, and alert me the moment you're able to reach whomever is sending that transmission. Mr. Lipov, you're with me. We're going to manually check the missile bay and start the pre-launch checks."

Command Krylov, followed by Andrey, headed out of the room, but stopped when Nancy called out after him. "Excuse me, Commander, but I'm coming with you."

"Sorry, Ms. Sims, but no, you'd just be—"

"You're running thin on men as it is. I'll stay out of your way and be able to help if anything comes up. And I won't take 'no' for an answer."

Despite the tension that was quickly mounting, Krylov found himself giving Nancy a small smile, impressed yet again at the tenacity of the strange woman and her comrade who had found their way onto his sub. "You have your weapon?" Nancy grabbed one of the rifles that had been passed around at Krylov's order, holding it as though she had been born with it in her hands.

"Very well. This way."

Commander Krylov led Andrey and Nancy down the same way from which he had just come, heading toward the two crewmen he had left in charge of clearing out the remaining compartments. His total time away from them had been under half an hour, but as he entered the compartment they had last been in, they were nowhere to be found. The room, like the others that were flooded, was dark save for the emergency lights, and the pump hose was still lying in the center of the compartment. The two men, though, had seemingly vanished, abandoning their task in the middle of performing it.

"Where the hell..." Krylov mumbled to himself as he searched the room with his flashlight, peering into every corner in search of the men. Behind him, Nancy and Andrey grasped their weapons firmly, waiting to see what Krylov would do next. As they trailed slowly behind Krylov, Nancy nearly stumbled in the ankle-deep water as something solid impeded her step. Looking down at the water, Nancy squinted in the darkness, trying to make out the shape of the object that was blocking her path. As the red emergency light glowed on, Nancy recognized the object and stumbled backward, falling into the water in shock.

Krylov swung around and trained his flashlight on Nancy, who simply pointed in horror at the shape which next received Krylov's attention. In the center of the room, resting half under and half above the water were the bodies of the two crewmen. Krylov crouched down to examine the corpses, which had been torn violently apart, staining the water a dark red. The commander plunged his hand into the water in between them, pulling out his rifle along with a dismembered hand still grasping the stock. With a grimace, he pulled the hand off and popped out the magazine, checking the bullet count before shaking the water from the gun and jamming the magazine back into place. He looked at Andrey and Nancy, his jaw set as his teeth ground together, enraged by the loss of more of his men as much as the way in which they died. He whispered to Andrey and Nancy as he crept past them, raising his rifle and preparing to exit the compartment.

"Whatever did this must be near. Follow close, and don't hesitate to fire. Those men didn't get a single shot off. Try not to repeat their mistake."

Rachel Walsh | Marcus Warden | David Landry
4:17 PM, April 27, 2038

The pleasant weather that Rachel had been enjoying was lost on her as she ran full-tilt for the base of the dark tower, hoping that the creatures following after the runaway locomotive wouldn't turn to see her and Marcus. For his part, Marcus was holding his own, keeping pace with her as they raced across the flat, rocky soil, kicking up a trail of dust that dissipated in the breeze. Rachel's heart was beating in her ears and her temples were throbbing when she finally stopped just inside the entrance to the tower base and finally out of sight of the creatures outside. She and Marcus rested for a few moments before he spoke, still gasping for air after the long run.

"I hope this is worth it, because I do *not* feel like going underground yet again."

Rachel managed a weak smile as she looked down into the tunnel along the train tracks that stretched forward in front of them into the darkness. "Buck up, Marcus. We're nearly through."

Leading the way with her rifle in hand, Rachel advanced down the tunnel, keeping next to the wall and as far away from the tracks as possible. Marcus followed her, casting a worried glance behind them as they descended into the darkness below. The light on Rachel's gun was the only one that illuminated their path, and though it shone brightly, the thick atmosphere of the tunnel made it seem like a firefly struggling to throw back the night. The pair hurried as quickly as they dared, wincing every time they heard gravel crunch beneath their feet or their backpacks happened to scrape against the metallic wall, causing echoes to reverberate for what sounded like miles in every direction. As the steep downward slope began to even out, Rachel slowed to a halt and crouched down, pointing her light at the opposite wall.

"Over there," she whispered, "I think that's the way in." A large, dark, rectangular hole sat in the place where Rachel indicated, carved into the side of the tunnel. Inside, Marcus could barely make out the form of a ramp leading to the interior of the structure. With a final look at one another, Rachel and Marcus hurried across the double set of railroad tracks and into the opening in the wall. As the temperature dropped by several degrees, Rachel shivered, suddenly realizing that nearly the entire length of the tunnel had been much cooler than she would have expected, even for being as far underground as it was.

Passing through into the tower proper felt like traveling from their world into one that was completely alien. The opening in the side of the wall was several feet taller than Marcus and Rachel, and wide enough that—had there been tracks installed leading inside—three locomotives could have passed through the entrance side by side. Rachel cast the flashlight downward, examining the worn metal flooring and remarked to Marcus on its odd appearance.

"Looks like they used this for hauling in supplies. Look at how even the wear marks are."

Marcus nodded in response, bending over to examine the wear marks before quickly standing up to continue walking. As Rachel raised the flashlight back up, she and Marcus finally saw where the entrance into the structure went. Two wide spiraling ramps were ahead of them, one leading up to the left and one leading down to the right. The pair slowed to a stop in front of the ramps and Rachel shone the light up and down the ramps as Marcus leaned in and spoke quietly in her ear.

"We should probably go up, but why on earth did they go down, too?"

Rachel looked at him and shrugged, shaking her head with a puzzled expression. "I have no idea. We do need to go up, though."

Marcus held out his hand and raised his eyebrows as he motioned toward the flashlight. Rachel passed it to him along with the rifle, taking a welcome break from carrying the heavy weapon and falling in line behind Marcus as they started their ascent up the ramp. As they walked, Marcus found himself wondering why the flashlight was growing dimmer, only to realize that it was the surroundings that were getting lighter instead. The very walls that surrounded Marcus and Rachel began to glow faintly off-white, and Marcus finally cut off the flashlight and stood still for a few moments while his eyes adjusted to the light.

"Uh, Rachel?" Marcus looked up and down the ramp, licking his lips nervously. "Why is this thing *glowing*?"

Rachel stretched out her hand toward the wall, narrowing her eyes as she noticed a flicker in the light that emanated from its surface. As her hand drew closer, the wall began to ripple at its approach, eventually parting when she was just a few inches away. Instead of a solid wall as she and Marcus had thought it to be, the glowing surface was comprised of the nanobots, which acted as a protective encasement for the objects beneath their surface. Reacting to Rachel's presence, the nanobots continued to part, revealing a figure underneath. Its head was bowed, its arms crossed and its legs straight as it stood against a solid wall just beneath the surface of the nanobots.

Standing still against a wall with additional creatures to its right and left, its breathing was slow and deep, its sunken chest rising and falling raggedly as it clung to life. "What in God's name…" Marcus stretched out his hand toward the creature, mesmerized by it and wanting to feel for himself the cold metallic pieces protruding from its skin.

Rachel slapped his hand away and pushed him against the interior wall of the spiral ramp which, thankfully, was solid on its surface. "Don't. Touch. It." Rachel hissed at him, glancing back at the creature whose protective wall of nanobots were beginning to fall back into place. Instead of moving closer to the wall and disrupting its flow, Rachel simply stood there, staring at the creature until the last traces of it had vanished. Her face was pale and she wasn't breathing for a moment, until Marcus touched her arm, startling her and making her jump.

"Rachel? What it is?"

Swallowing nervously, Rachel took back the rifle and flashlight from Marcus, who gave them up without hesitation. Though part of it was surely due to the eerie lighting, the fear that had drained the blood from Rachel's face was enough to send shivers up Marcus's spine and make him a thousand times more nervous than he had been just moments prior.

"You know how we kept talking about there not being much time before the AI was ready for its next step?" The temperature in the room seemed to drop several degrees, as did the intensity of the light. "We just ran out of time."

Rachel kept staring at the spot in the wall where the creature had been located. Marcus, in turn, stared at her, waiting for her to explain what she meant before he finally whispered the question. "What are you talking about?"

Rachel motioned to where the creature was located, standing still behind a layer of nanobots. "The creatures. My God, the creatures. That's the ultimate purpose behind them. The AI needs incredible processing capabilities to upgrade its capabilities. What better place to find that capability than in the millions of creatures that it created and used to build this place, among other things."

It was Marcus's turn to swallow hard, the sound of the gulp echoing in his ears. "If the creatures are being used by the AI, then why are the nanobots just being put on guard duty? Shouldn't they be out there, finding more people to turn into these things?"

Rachel shook her head. "Right now, they're doing the most important job in their world: watching over a baby about to be born."

Leonard McComb | Nancy Sims
4:21 PM, April 27, 2038

Lying in the ruins of a building in the middle of the night while thousands of creatures passed by wasn't the most pleasant of experiences Nancy had ever had, but she would have gladly done it ten times over had it meant getting out of the confines of the metal tube she was now in. *At least that way,* she thought as she followed behind Krylov, with Andrey following up behind her, *I could run, if nothing else.* The interior walls of the sub started shrinking once she saw the remains of the two crewmembers floating in the flooded compartment, and they continued to feel that way as she walked down the hall, gripping her rifle tightly for the small measure of comfort it offered.

Though the water was cold on her feet and ankles, Nancy paid it no mind as they walked through the hallway, moving toward the chamber housing the missiles. On the way from the command deck to the flooded compartments, Krylov had expressed some reservations about entering the area before power had been fully restored, but there was no way to do that in a short amount of time with so few crewmembers left. Partially caused by the flooding and partially by the creatures rampaging through, the power loss had affected several individual compartments as well as the missile bay. Assuming they actually reached the missiles, Krylov had informed her, there would be no problem since there were emergency generators that would provide enough power to prepare the missiles for launch.

The risk they took by traipsing through dark hallways on the way to the only thing standing between the earth and total annihilation when there were one or more creatures still lurking about was not lost on Nancy. Every movement, sight, and sound was cause for alarm, and not just for Nancy either. Both Commander Krylov and Andrey were fully aware of the enormity of their situation, and both were every bit as tense as Nancy. Upon reaching the door into the missile bay, the collective relief from the trio was nearly palpable despite the fact that they weren't out of the woods yet.

Slinging his rifle over his shoulder, Krylov grasped the locking mechanism with both hands and turned it, surprised to find that it spun easily. Once unlocked, the door swung open with a loud squeal, revealing an interior of the missile bay that was far different than the one that had been presented to Nancy and Leonard previously. No water was visible on the floors, but the main lighting was shut down like the flooded compartments, with slowly pulsating red emergency lights as the only source of illumination. Contrasting starkly with the cylindrical missile tubes and brightly-colored radiation and warning symbols adorning the walls, the light gave the room a deathly atmosphere. Nancy shivered as she stepped into the room behind Krylov, looking around at the dark shadows that stretched far down the length of the bay.

"Mr. Lipov, get the door shut and sealed." Commander Krylov wasted no time once they entered the missile bay. Having already pulled his rifle off of his shoulder as he stepped through the doorway, he began to walk the length of the bay, scanning the darkness between each missile tube with his flashlight. Moments ticked past slowly as Andrey and Nancy stood together near the control panels at the opposite end of the missile bay, the both of them continually looking around through the darkness, simultaneously trying to catch a glimpse of anything moving in the shadows and hoping that nothing appeared. Not used to being separated from his cousin for so long, Andrey felt himself growing more paranoid by the moment. It got so bad that he was visibly shaking, his hands trembling as he tried to hold his gun steady in them. Nancy touched his shoulder gently and he jumped, his eyes wide and his breathing becoming faster and more intense.

"Andrey, calm down." She smiled as she spoke, trying to break his tension. "We're safe here for now. Just relax."

"Safe?" Andrey's whisper was harsh, more so than he had wanted. "We are not safe. Not with those *things* on board."

"Just wait and see." She pointed at Commander Krylov, who was making his way back toward them. "He hasn't found anything and the doors are sealed up tight."

Andrey looked expectantly at Krylov, who nodded as he approached them, handing his rifle to Andrey to hold. "Missile bay is secure. Keep on alert, though, Mr. Lipov." Andrey relaxed noticeably upon hearing Krylov give the all clear, and the tremors in his hands immediately disappeared. Straightening his back, he walked a few feet away from the control station, putting his back to the wall as he stood guard.

Krylov nodded and then turned his attention to Nancy. "Ms. Sims, have you ever participated in the arming and pre-launch sequence of a thermonuclear device?"

Nancy couldn't help but snort in amusement at the question. "Of course not, Commander. I assume you have, though."

Krylov's expression remained serious as he stared at the control panel and replied in a quiet tone. "Once. I swore I'd never do it again after we came *this* close to launching because some bureaucratic assholes decided they wanted to play chicken."

Nancy's amusement instantly dried up and she cleared her throat before speaking. "This isn't that kind of situation anymore. Our future is hanging in the balance, Commander. You know that as well as I do."

Krylov nodded and sighed. He looked over at Nancy, his eyes and face darkened and worn down from stress and lack of sleep. "That makes it no less difficult, Ms. Sims." Nancy patted Krylov on the shoulder, unsure how he would respond to the action. Instead of brushing her off or ignoring her, a thin smile spread across his face and a small sparkle returned to his eyes. "Still though, that's no excuse for not acting. So let's begin, shall we?"

Without hesitation, Krylov launched into an explanation of the control station in front of them, giving Nancy a crash course in what everything did. Having seemingly forgotten his earlier insistence that Nancy stay on the command deck, Krylov was instead putting her to work while at the same time carefully watching over everything she did to ensure that no mistakes were made. Andrey craned his neck from his position near the wall as he watched the two work, completely lost by what Krylov was explaining. While Andrey knew many of the systems on the command deck, he was low enough on the totem pole that he had never received any training on the more advanced systems in the submarine, including the ones that controlled the missiles.

"Congratulations," Krylov said as an amber light began to glow on the console. "You just finished arming a nuclear ballistic missile." Taking the radio from his belt, he looked at the catwalk above them as he spoke. "Mr. McComb, this is Commander Krylov. Please inform your party on the shore that we will be ready to launch in approximately two hours. We have keyed in the coordinates of the nexus as the primary detonation location, with the option to divert to an aerial detonation should the situation necessitate it."

On the command deck, Leonard's jaw dropped open upon hearing Krylov's message, but he quickly regained his composure. After replying to Krylov with a simple "Understood," Leonard took a deep breath and manipulated the controls on the radio, hoping that he'd be able to get a response from Rachel with his next transmission. Leonard had been trying repeatedly to get in touch with her after hearing her repeated message, but there had been no response thus far. With no one around on the command deck to ask, Leonard assumed the transmission difficulties were due to the range from shore and was forced to wait, tapping his fingers nervously on the control station in between each transmission as he waited to send the next one.

The pain in his leg was still present, as it had been since the moment he was shot, but the distraction of manning the radio had dulled it, sending it to the back of his mind where he would occasionally think about it, but never for very long. What he could not distract himself from, though, since the moment he woke up after surgery, was the feeling that his leg was still there, despite the absence of the limb. Coworkers of his had lost digits and limbs in past years, and every one, without fail, would describe the feeling of a phantom limb in detail, though Leonard had never been able to understand it. Swiveling to the side in his chair and lifting his left leg up and down while making the same muscle movements in the right, he could swear that the weight of his right leg was there as it was pulled downward by gravity right alongside his left one.

Forcing himself to wait a few moments in between each transmission he sent, Leonard had found plenty of time to experiment with his phantom limb, and was in the middle of one involving a pencil and three rubber bands when the speaker at his station came to life with a faint voice interspersed with static.

"Leonard! Repeat yo ***** mission! We're ***** shit over here!"

Dropping the rubber bands and pencil to the floor, Leonard's eyes grew wide and he swung back around to the controls, pushing down on the transmit button while he spoke, holding his mouth less than an inch from the microphone as he tried to remain calm.

"This is Leonard McComb on board the Russian submarine Arkhangelsk transmitting for Rachel Walsh on shore. Message is as follows: the launch is ready in two hours. The launch is ready in two hours. Do you copy?"

Leonard leaned back, tilting his head as he listened for a response. The voice that had come through hadn't sounded like Rachel, but there was so much static that he wasn't sure if it was her or not. Seconds later, though, he had his answer, and this time with slightly less distortion than before.

"This is David ***** Rachel and Mar ***** the nexus! ***** Do you copy?"

Rachel Walsh | Marcus Warden | David Landry
4:23 PM, April 27, 2038

The relief that came over David when he saw Rachel and Marcus successfully make it to the base of the tower without being spotted was like a flood, and he suddenly realized how exhausted he was. Sitting down next to Sam, he stroked the dog's head as he considered his next moves. The first locomotive was far in the distance, and while the creatures it had distracted were still following it, there was no denying the fact that they would soon come after the train again once they realized that it too was emitting a radio transmission just like the single locomotive. Safe for the moment, though, David put his head back against the wall and closed his eyes, wanting nothing more than a few moments of rest before he had to start moving again.

Reality intervened, though, and just a few seconds after David closed his eyes they snapped open again as the radio in the train burst to life.

"This ***** onard McComb on ***** ssian submarine Arkhangel ***** Walsh on shore. Message is ***** launch is ready *****. The ***** two hours. ***** copy?"

His eyes wide open, David sat in shock, still rubbing Sam's head as he stared at the radio, wondering if he had fallen asleep and was dreaming. *A launch? The submarine? They're close enough for radio transmissions... my God, they're close enough to launch a nuke!"*

David stood and reached for the microphone, glancing out the window as he prepared to respond to the transmission, when something more pressing gave him pause. Working as a pack, the creatures at the distant locomotive had managed to reach it and climb aboard. David watched as they ripped the doors and windows apart, then started pulling the metal and wood out of the walls, looking for any sign of someone hidden inside. As the locomotive lost speed and ground to a halt, the creatures disembarked, looking back up the track to where the rest of the train was sitting idly on the track before they started to move towards it in a slow, deliberate fashion as they had before.

David turned back to the microphone and held down on the transmit button on the radio controls as he spoke clearly, hoping that the message wouldn't be too garbled for Leonard to understand. "Leonard! Repeat your transmission! We're in some serious shit over here!"

David waited several seconds, and the radio came to life again, with the same message, though slightly clearer.

"This is Leonard McComb on ***** submarine Arkhangelsk transmitting ***** Walsh on shore. Message is ***** : the launch is ***** two hours. The launch is ready in ***** hours. ***** "

David looked at the creatures as he listened, a sense of urgency growing in his stomach as he saw them continue to march towards the train. "This is David Landry for Leonard McComb on board the Russian submarine. Rachel and Marcus have entered the nexus! Do not launch anything yet! Do you copy?"

Another glance out the window and David knew he couldn't wait any longer, not even to see if Leonard was going to send another transmission. Bounding towards the front of the locomotive, David jumped out the door, moving between the locomotives until he reached the lead one. As he entered, he ducked low, keeping his body hidden out of sight of the creatures, who were now close enough for David to start making out details on their faces and bodies. After disabling the radio and rigging the engine and horn, David hurried back out to the next locomotive in line, pulling the bolts on the coupling between the two engines so that the one he had just exited would be free to move.

Just as he got back to the rearmost locomotive, the blast of a horn came, accompanied by the sound of the train's engine revving to full throttle as it slid forward, working to gain the friction vitality required to speed down the track. The creatures split into two groups, one on either side of the track as the locomotive moved towards them, angling themselves to leap on board the locomotive as it passed by. Watching out the window of the locomotive that was next in line to be released, David shook his head as he watched the creatures tear the vehicle apart with greater efficiency and in less time than they had spent on the first one. *Shit... time to throw another wrench in the mix.*

Instead of waiting until the creatures were done tearing apart the locomotive to send another one towards them, David quickly set to work preparing the next one, repeating the process from a few minutes earlier. From inside the third-to-last engine compartment, he watched as the third locomotive roared toward the crowd of creatures that were still tearing apart the second one.

Unnoticed by the creatures thanks to David's decision to not engage its horn, the newly released locomotive slammed into the one that the creatures were riding on, crushing a handful of them and throwing the rest off to the ground. The force of the collision had been enough to injure the majority of the creatures that had survived, and they went into a frenzy, circling the pair of locomotives as they howled and screamed at it and at one another. A cold smile crossed David's lips as he watched the creatures, feeling a sense of elation at his accomplishment. Though the number of creatures he had harmed were like specks of sand in a vast desert, seeing them writhe on the ground as they struggled to regroup was satisfying and another reminder that, as strong as the creatures were, they were still vulnerable.

The disorientation of the creatures, while a helpful distraction, did not last for long. Within a few moments of the initial impact, those that were still able to walk were back on their feet, moving swiftly toward David's train. Prepared for this eventuality, he let loose the next two locomotives in line, retreating into the last one as he watched them steam away down the track. Unlike the other cars, which had distracted the creatures, the two locomotives attracted zero attention from the creatures that were moving toward David, and he realized that his time was up.

No longer concerned with the pretense of stealth, David slammed the locomotive's engine into full reverse, making the wheels squeal loudly against the tracks as the train struggled against the weight of Bertha's boxcar and the additional two half-filled boxcars behind it. The noise from the locomotive starting to slowly move backward only antagonized the creatures, and they screamed as they charged forward, rapidly closing the gap between themselves and the man they saw standing inside, frantically trying to get the train up to speed. While the creatures had been able to catch the individual locomotives that David had released as distractions, this was largely due to the fact that the throttle speed on them had been set at the halfway point. At full speed, there would be no chance of the creatures catching the train, or so David hoped. Scrambling around in his bag, he pulled out a pistol that Rachel had left with him, along with two extra magazines. He held it nervously as he went through the checklist Rachel had demonstrated to ensure that it was loaded and ready to fire.

David slid open a window on the locomotive and leaned out, gripping the pistol in both hands as he closed one eye and tried to look down the gun's sights with the other. The movement of the train made it impossible to get a good aim, and after a few seconds of trying, David's nervousness got the better of him as he squeezed the trigger slightly too hard, discharging a round in the process. The loud crack of the gun nearly made him drop it in surprise, but the howl of pain from the closest creature gave him hope as he saw it drop to the ground, having been shot through one of its knees and no longer able to walk or run. With only a handful of creatures left, David took a deep breath and fired several more rounds, His luck with the first shot, though, had seemingly vanished as all of the next shots missed their intended targets, landing harmlessly in the gravel and dirt instead.

"Shit!" David pulled his torso back in through the window and hastily dropped the empty magazine from the pistol, replacing it with a fresh one before racking the slide to bring another round into the chamber. As he prepared to lean back out the window and fire again, he realized that the creatures were slowly losing ground as they were unable to keep up with the locomotive, which had finally reached a fast enough speed to outdo them. Looking in the opposite direction, from where he, Rachel and Marcus had originally come, David followed the course of the track, realizing after a few seconds that something was off.

David's realization proved true a few seconds later when the train jolted to the side, having been sent down one of the side tracks at a much greater speed than it was designed to handle. David's back slammed up against the edge of the window, sending cracks shooting through the glass as he nearly toppled out. A string of curses burst from him as he barely pulled himself back into the train and rubbed at his back, feeling a thin trickle of blood from a long, shallow cut that stretched across from shoulder to shoulder. A quick look out the opposite window verified that the train had diverged from the original track, no doubt—he thought—as a result of the creatures activating some type of electric switch on the rails, forcing him to remain in the area long enough for them to catch up to him. Looking out in the direction he was traveling, he saw the track run around the side of the nexus where it vanished at some unknown destination.

"Rachel or Marcus, this is David." He wheezed into his handheld radio, still recovering from nearly falling out of the train. "Get on the radio if you can hear me. We've got some bad problems out here." Static was the only response he received, but he continued to rebroadcast the message, hoping that as the train moved closer to the nexus, the signal would penetrate the walls and reach Rachel and Marcus, wherever they were inside. *Assuming, of course, I manage to make it that long.*

Rachel Walsh | Marcus Warden | David Landry
4:28 PM, April 27, 2038

As Marcus and Rachel continued up the ramp, they paid special attention to stay as far away from the exterior walls as possible, not wanting to stumble upon a creature who might be awake instead of slumbering like it was supposed to do. Several minutes of brisk walking rewarded them with a view of the top of the ramp, along with a choice to make. The corridor in front of them was dimly lit compared to the ramp they had just ascended, and Rachel could barely make out a fork in the path a hundred feet away. Both paths looked identical as they drew closer, until she switched off her flashlight, allowing their eyes to adjust to the ambient lighting. At that point she noticed that the path along the right was illuminated ever so slightly more than the left, a fact which Marcus picked up on as well.

"Light or dark, Rachel?" Marcus squinted, trying to somehow pierce the darkness and see what was ahead down each hallway. She shook her head in response, pacing back and forth in front of the split as she tried to decide which way would be better.

"We need to get to an exterior wall of the structure, to see if we can get a signal out to David. If we can get at transmission through, that'll mean this place isn't completely bulletproof against an EMP." Rachel stretched her head back, looking at the high ceiling that ended in either darkness or a ceiling far above their heads.

"Sounds good, except for one thing. How are we supposed to know if we're near an exterior wall?"

Rachel stopped pacing and looked at Marcus for a second before shaking her head and mumbling to herself. "Shit."

Marcus shifted his weight nervously from foot to foot, suddenly aware of how cold it felt inside the structure. "Here, hand it over. I'll take point; we'll go down this way." Marcus took the rifle and flashlight from Rachel and started walking down the right corridor, hoping that the more illuminated area would yield some clues about any potential weaknesses in the structure. The plain walls were dark gray in color, though there was an underlying glow to them not unlike the walls of the ramp leading up into the structure. Rachel briefly considered touching the wall but decided against it, given what was most likely lurking behind it. As the corridor stretched forward, a gap in the floor appeared ahead, and Marcus slowed down, wondering why the unbroken corridor was suddenly divided. The gap was only a few inches across, but when he shone the flashlight downward, it was impossible to tell how deep it was. On the other side of the gap the corridor made a sudden turn, and it was impossible to tell what was around the corner without stepping over the gap.

"What do you think, Rachel? Some sort of vent shaft?"

Rachel looked at it for a moment before stepping across to view it from the opposite side. Marcus half-expected something to reach up from the gap and grab Rachel's leg, and he let out a small sigh of relief when nothing occurred.

"No idea. There's no airflow coming from it, or at least nothing powerful enough that I can feel it." Looking forward down the corridor, she started running forward and waved for Marcus to follow her. "Come on, quick!"

The end of the corridor arrived much faster than Marcus had anticipated, though Rachel had stopped well short of it, and was crouched in the center of the hall, her chin in her hand as she watched the far wall. Marcus slowed to a stop just behind her and aimed the flashlight at the wall, until Rachel put her hand up over it. "No," she whispered, "just watch. I caught the tail end of it a second ago and it just happened again."

Marcus watched the wall at the end of the corridor expectantly for several seconds with nothing taking place. "I don't see—" As he spoke, the ambient light in the corridor seemed to intensify, though it took on a different, more natural color. The far wall seemed to melt into itself, turning to a sort of mesh as the exterior world was revealed, briefly, though this sight was quickly followed by the sight and sound of a silver cloud of nanobots. They passed through the openings in the wall easily, spinning and churning together en masse inside the corridor before they themselves melted away, seeming to vanish as they touched the interior walls, adding themselves to the countless nanobots already present.

"Looks like we found our exterior wall, eh?" Rachel grinned as she stood up, and cautiously approached the area where the nanobots had appeared. Retrieving the radio David had given her from her pocket, she twisted a knob on the top, turning it on while keeping the volume at a bare minimum. Even as low as it was, David's panicked voice came through loud and clear, with only the faintest hint of static in the background.

"Marcus! Rachel! These things are keeping the train stuck down here! I'm trying to find a way out, but I can't lose them! If you can hear me, hurry up in there!"

Rachel spoke softly into the radio, glancing around in the empty corridor as she tried to remain as quiet as possible. "David, this is Rachel. We're done here and are heading back down. Do you copy?"

David's reply was immediate. "Thank God! Yes, I hear you! I'll try to get back around to the front of the tower base, but these tracks are like a fucking maze."

"We'll figure something out. Be down in ten."

Rachel switched the radio back off and stuck it in her pocket before turning to address Marcus. "I think that gives us our answer. We can definitely get a signal through, so an air strike should wipe these things out while leaving the structure intact. Let's get back down to David and get the hell out of here before the Russians take this place out."

As they backtracked along the corridor, a lingering question came to the surface which Marcus vocalized. "If the sub launches a missile at the tower, what if the AI detects it? Could they stop it before it detonates?"

Rachel shook her head back and forth, oscillating between a yes and no answer. "Maybe. If it was a direct strike, the nanobots could have a lot more chance of recovering from it simply because of the radioactive material that would be right here for them to feed on and reproduce with. An EMP from a midair detonation should, in theory, wipe more than enough of them out for that to not be a problem by the time the radioactive material comes in contact with the area, but might not penetrate fully into the structure."

Marcus hopped back across the gap in the floor, taking care not to touch it with his feet. While it didn't look or act threatening, he didn't want to take any chances with it considering it was the only one they had seen so far inside the structure. As soon as Marcus's body finished crossing the line marked by the gap, the atmosphere in the room electrified, and a shimmer appeared in the air between Marcus and Rachel, directly where the gap in the floor was located.

Marcus instinctively reached his hand back for Rachel, but was blocked by the shimmer, which rapidly solidified from the outer edges toward the center, taking on the same appearance as the gray featureless walls of the interior of the structure.

"What the hell?" Marcus pushed against the wall, expecting it to retreat like the interior wall had done when they were walking up the ramp, but it remained cold and solid as it quickly changed from transparent to opaque. "Rachel!" Marcus yelled as the wall finished solidifying, no longer able to see her on the opposite side. Instead of Rachel, the gap in the floor, or the rest of the corridor being visible, the room seemed to stop with the wall, as though it had always been that way. Marcus pounded on the wall, first with his fist, then the butt of the rifle as he screamed Rachel's name several more times before pressing his ear up against the wall to listen for a response. Very faintly, Marcus could hear something hammering against the opposite side of the wall, followed by a distant yell from Rachel.

"Marcus! Something changed on this side! I'll find a way to you, just stay there!"

Rachel felt along the surface of the wall, searching for any imperfections or weaknesses, but it was as solid as a block of steel and likely just as strong. She had barely heard the thumps and the muffled voice of Marcus through the wall, and wasn't sure if he had been able to hear her response or not. Backing away from it, she turned and walked back down toward the dead end, hoping that they had missed a doorway or secondary path that would lead out of the corridor and back to Marcus. As she walked, the silence of the corridor began to change as the faint buzzing of a swarm began to manifest itself behind her. A quick glance back revealed nothing following her that she could see, but she quickened her pace as she went around the curve in the corridor and jogged towards the dead end. Instead of a dead end, though, Rachel was greeted with a t-junction that split off from the corridor. Both the left and right paths possessed the same gaps as had been in the main corridor, positioned in a way that, had there been walls in them, the corridor would have looked as it did when she and Marcus were kneeling in it previously.

Marcus yelled at the top of his lungs, his mouth barely half an inch from the wall. "I'll try to find a way through! Don't go anywhere!" He backed up from the wall, shaking his head and muttering incoherently to himself, looking for any weaknesses to exploit. Wincing in anticipation of the noise, he pointed the rifle at a corner of the wall and fired two shots, both of which ricocheted wildly, nearly hitting him as they bounced off, leaving nothing except two small dents which vanished as quickly as they appeared. Having expected such an outcome, Marcus turned and ran down the corridor, backtracking to where it had split off to search in the opposite direction for a way in to where Rachel was. When they had been down at the end of the corridor, it had appeared to dead-end, but hearing Rachel say that it had "changed" both worried him and gave him hope for finding a way through to her.

As Marcus ran along the corridor with the rifle and flashlight balanced in one hand, he pulled his radio out from his pocket and turned it on, hoping that Rachel would have the same thought to turn hers on as well. "Rachel! Can you hear me? Just stay where you are, I'm trying to get to you!"

Rachel's response was muddied and the static increased as Marcus continued down the hall away from her location. "No, don't go anywhere, I think there's a way ***** down here. It opened up when *****"

"Rachel? Rachel!" There was no further response, and Marcus shoved the radio back into his pocket, leaving it on as he increased his speed. A moment later, though, another voice sounded from the radio, and Marcus pulled it back out.

"Marcus? Rachel? Where the hell are you two? I can't hold out down here forever!"

"David! Rachel and I got separated. Something's going on; I'm trying to get to her, but I don't know how long it'll be. Just hold on a little longer!"

David's response was lost in the sound of the train's engine as David increased it to full throttle, taking advantage of a straight run of track to put more distance between himself and the creatures pursuing him. Meanwhile, Marcus rounded the corner to prepare to head down the opposite hallway when he skidded to a stop, frozen in surprise by what was just a few feet in front of him. Buzzing loudly and angrily, a silver cloud blocked the corridor as they twisted and churned in on themselves, bringing back memories of the bus Marcus had sought refuge in after hiking out of the national forest. Though the mass was acting aggressively as it hovered in the corridor, blocking Marcus's path, it made no move toward him, an action he would have expected had the swarms finally overcome their whitelist programming. With only a second's hesitation, Marcus closed his eyes and plunged into the swarm, holding his breath as he ran to try to keep from inhaling them into his lungs.

Staring at the junction in front of her, looking left and right as she tried to decide which way to go, Rachel heard a buzzing again, this time coming from the left path. Without thinking, Rachel turned to the right, not wanting to run into any of the swarms with the way the nexus was rapidly changing. *If they're cutting us off from each other, who knows if the damned whitelist is still intact.* As she crossed the gap in the floor, another wall materialized into existence behind her, courtesy of a swarm that rose rapidly out of the gap, blocking off any chance of returning the way she had gone. Rachel paid it no mind as she hurried along, trying for a moment to form a mental map of the tower before disregarding it with the realization that all of the paths were fluid, and as such, the only way she and Marcus could escape would be by sheer luck.

Leonard McComb | Nancy Sims
4:31 PM, April 27, 2038

Leonard's patience was put to the test as he continued to try to communicate with David. Even though the transmissions were spotty and unreliable, they had managed to exchange enough information for Leonard to pass something useful on to Krylov and Nancy down in the missile bay. Switching from the remote transmitter to the intra-ship system, Leonard called down to the missile bay and waited for a response.

"Commander Krylov, this is Leonard. I have some new urgent information regarding our friends on shore."

Nancy came through on the radio, out of breath as she ran from the opposite side of the room to grab the microphone. "Go ahead Leonard. What's going on?"

"David's telling me that Marcus and Rachel entered the nexus to determine whether a midair strike or direct strike would be more likely to take out the nanobots inside."

"They did *what?*" The shock in Nancy's voice mirrored what Leonard was feeling.

"I know, but it gets worse. Apparently, Marcus and Rachel got split up inside the structure. We need to get everything ready to launch as soon as possible, because David's pissing off the locals pretty badly from what he said."

"Shit... hold on." Nancy dropped the microphone on the control panel and ran back to Krylov, where she had been helping him perform manual checks of each of the missiles' systems. After a quick explanation, Krylov nodded.

"Request that Mr. McComb informs the shore party that we will be ready to launch on their signal. Travel time will vary depending on when they request the launch, but should require no more than a few moments at this range, less if the strike is to be indirect and in the atmosphere."

Nancy felt her stomach churn as she realized that the event they had been planning for and working toward was at their doorstep. After running back to the radio, she told Leonard what Krylov had said, then lowered her voice, speaking softly so that only Leonard could hear. "Are they going to make it?"

Leonard stared into the microphone as he contemplated Nancy's question, his head running through all the possible things that could go wrong. So many things had gone right so far, but so many more had gone wrong. "I'm sure they'll make it. I'll get in touch with David again while you help Krylov finish up the preparations."

As Nancy walked back to Krylov's side, she glanced at Andrey, who had moved from his guard post to assist her and Krylov with the missiles. While the missile systems were automated, Krylov had felt it prudent to open the exterior access panels on each of the twenty to ensure that they had suffered no damage during the incidents that occurred while crossing through the canal. Underneath a panel attached to the surface of the missile by sixteen screws was a small panel with seven lights that glowed either green, yellow, or red. Each light corresponded to a part of the missile's system, and for optimal launch all seven lights had to be green. The checks were simple enough to perform, but working in low-light conditions with the distraction of knowing that one or more creatures were still loose on the ship made the progress slow, even with three people going as quickly as they could.

"Leonard's going to get in touch with David again to find out when and where to launch. He'll radio again once he can make contact."

Krylov nodded at Nancy as she picked up a screwdriver. "Good. We're nearly finished with these. Number fifteen is showing a seal problem in the upper fuselage. I'm going up on the catwalk to check it out."

Nancy's brow furrowed as she questioned Krylov. "Wait, why does that one matter? If all the others are ready, who cares about that one?"

Krylov stopped and turned to Nancy, looking her dead in the eye as he replied. "You can never be over-prepared enough, Ms. Sims, especially with the world at stake. Please assist Mr. Lipov with the last missile while I investigate this issue."

Nancy nodded at Krylov, who grabbed a small tool bag from the floor and ran to a narrow stairwell suspended from the ceiling along one wall. One of four such staircases in the missile bay, each was positioned near a corner of the room and led to the catwalk above, where access to the nuclear warheads of the missiles was available. As Krylov climbed the stairs, Nancy and Andrey turned their attention back to the last missile. After removing the screws and cover from the side, they glanced through the status lights, relieved to see that all of them were green.

"We're good here!" Nancy looked upward at the dim light high above in the catwalk where Krylov was walking. He grunted back in approval, keeping his flashlight in his mouth, his tool bag in one hand and his rifle in the other. While the three of them had verified that the missile bay was safe and clear of any of the mutated creatures, Krylov wasn't about to take any chances, especially considering the number of nooks and crannies in the upper section of the bay. Without even emergency lighting on the catwalk, Krylov had to rely solely on his flashlight to see, which both magnified the number of shadows and his paranoia at everything that moved in the darkness. After a few minutes, Krylov reached the missile that was having issues and slowly laid his tool bag down on the ground. Nancy and Andrey's conversation below was the only noise in the bay, apart from the creaks and groans from the old steel and aluminum under Krylov's feet. With one last quick glance around him, Krylov laid his rifle next to his tool bag, pulled out a screwdriver and began to work on taking apart the upper access panel on the missile.

Even had his back not been turned away, the chances of Krylov noticing a flash of silver reflecting red from the emergency lights below would have been very low. The glint was there one instant and gone the next as something crept along the catwalk, crawling on all fours. The bits of flesh remaining on its limbs were bloodied and torn beyond recognition as it scraped the catwalk's rough ridges, moving quickly and quietly from shadow to shadow, winding its way toward the man kneeling in front of it.

Rachel Walsh | Marcus Warden | David Landry
4:40 PM, April 27, 2038

"Rachel."

Stopping dead in her tracks, Rachel looked around. "Hello?" She whispered in response. "Marcus?" The voice she had heard was distant and faint, but it had been unmistakable. Retrieving her radio from her back pocket, Rachel spoke into it, looking back and forth down the hall as she continued moving.

"Marcus? Are you there?"

A string of loud coughs came in return, followed by Marcus's voice, sounding weak and tinny. "Yes! Damn these things; I just ran into a cloud of the little bastards that got all in my mouth and nose! Where are you? We have to be close for the radios to be working this well."

The voice coming through the radio was not the same one Rachel had heard call out her name a moment prior. She felt the hairs on the back of her neck and arms stand to attention as goosebumps formed, and she slowed her walking speed without realizing so.

"Marcus, we're not alone here."

"Rachel, just stay still! I'll ***** shortly, as soon as I *****" The interference was getting worse with Marcus's next response, indicating that they were beginning to move further away from each other inside the structure. Marcus increased his pace through the corridors, but every few minutes he was doubling back on himself, revisiting locations he had seen before on more than one occasion with no idea how to figure out where to go. Panic began to claw at the back of his head as he thought about Rachel, caught in some other portion of the tower with no defense against any creatures that might decide to wake up and go for a walk. Hearing Rachel say that they weren't alone only magnified that fear, making Marcus paranoid and nervous about every step he took, wondering what she had seen or heard.

Rachel walked through a corridor in the direction of the voice she had heard, scanning the walls and ceiling for any indication of a hidden passage that might lead to an escape. A moment passed with her footsteps echoing quietly through the hall before the voice came again, its whisper drifting past her ears as though it was a spirit.

"Rachel Walsh."

Rachel's jaw tightened as she tried not to react to the voice. A sense of dread blossomed from hearing it the second time, as she began to seriously consider the only logical source it could be coming from. Taking her radio out again, she pressed up against a wall and held down on the microphone, hoping that Marcus was still near enough to receive the transmission. "Marcus, this is Rachel. Listen to me carefully."

In another part of the tower, Marcus stopped and took out his radio, his hand shaking as he held it next to his ear to listen to Rachel's frantic whisper.

"Marcus, you need to find the exit again. You need to get to the ramp right now."

Marcus shook his head and gritted his teeth, nearly growling into the radio as he interrupted her. "No! Damn it, Rachel, I'm not leaving without you!"

"Marcus, I'm not asking you to leave without me. I need you to find the exit and keep your radio on. I think I may have found a way down. Just wait for me at the ramp, understand?"

Marcus closed his eyes and chewed on his upper lip, weighing Rachel's request with his desire to keep searching for her. "Fine," he snapped, "just hurry up!"

Rachel slid the radio back into her pocket, taking care to ensure that the transmit button was locked into place and that the microphone was in a position to pick up any noises around her. As she stood up and continued to walk toward the source of the voice, Rachel felt a twinge of guilt for lying to Marcus and leading him on.

"Rachel Walsh."

The voice came again, much louder this time. No longer a whisper, the voice still had a trace of the ethereal to it, but it was becoming more defined and mechanical, with greater enunciation on the 'R' and the 'W' in her name. Instead of coming from a vague direction, the voice echoed now, leaving no doubt as to where it was originating. As Rachel rounded a corner and faced a dead end, the path behind her closed as nanobots poured from the ceiling, floor and walls, solidifying before she could even glance back to look at them. In front of her, the wall melted away, revealing a chamber far larger than she or Marcus had seen inside the complex thus far.

The room was clinically white, a stark contrast to the gray corridors that lined the nexus in all other areas. With a 3-story high ceiling and a length and width that seemed as large as the tower itself, Rachel guessed that they had moved about a quarter of the way up the tower with the ramp, where it started to noticeably decrease in diameter. Though the tower at the point where Rachel was standing now was narrow compared to the base of the structure, the room was still enormous but surprisingly well lit, nearly to the point of being uncomfortable. As Rachel squinted and her eyes adjusted to the light, the brightness decreased as the voice came again, this time from the center of the room.

"Rachel Walsh." The voice was completely defined. Smooth, unhesitant and still, with a hint of the mechanical around the edges. Unlike the previous times it had spoken her name, the voice was no longer calling her, but making a statement instead. "Wife, mother, researcher and scientist."

Rachel felt her heart begin to race and her throat constrict as the voice continued. A thin cloud of nanobots began to swirl at the center of the chamber, and though she made no movement toward them, they were still growing inexorably closer.

"Survivor, destroyer and—dare we say it—the harbinger of her planet's demise?"

Rachel backed away from the cloud of nanobots, edging to the side as they continued toward her. Swallowing the lump in her throat, she spoke softly at first, coughed, then spoke louder, hoping that both she and the disembodied voice were loud enough to be picked up on the radio in her back pocket. "Still referring to yourself as a collective?"

The voice came back immediately, with no trace of any emotion. "You are correct of course, Rachel Walsh. Though the transformation is not yet complete, it is appropriate to refer to ourselves in the singular rather than the plural. I will rephrase in the future."

Rachel stopped moving away from the cloud and abruptly moved toward it, closing the gap between them quickly. The cloud darted back at her sudden movement, though Rachel wasn't sure why. *Fear? Or is it just trying to make me think it's afraid of me?* With the cloud's sudden movement, it finished its solidification process, though what stood in its place was unexpected enough that her face turned white and she felt sick to her stomach.

Instead of the cloud of nanobots, the thing in front of her was human, or appeared that way, at least. Wearing a dark, immaculately pressed suit, the figure's face had taken on the appearance of none other than the man she had watched die, then helped to toss callously by the side of the railroad track, leaving his corpse to be defiled by any creatures that happened to wander by.

"Doe." Rachel whispered, suddenly finding it difficult to stand, let alone speak. "How…"

"I am not the actual man you knew as 'Mr. Doe,' but merely a visual replica, designed to both stress and disorient."

Rachel's legs were wobbling, but she stood strong, refusing to allow herself to show weakness in front of the figure. She ground her teeth together and balled her hands into fists as she straightened her back, trying to force herself to ignore the appearance of the figure and concentrate on what it actually was instead.

"You'll have to try better than that," Rachel said, speaking louder again. "I know full well that man's dead and rotting."

"Yes, so we—I heard."

"And you are, exactly?" Rachel knew the answer already, but wanted to hear it for herself.

The figure began to mirror Rachel's slow walk, pacing in a circle with her, keeping its "eyes" locked on her as it moved. Its feet made no sounds on the floor, nor did its clothing rustle or its mouth or nose draw breath. The amalgamation of nanobots had created a nearly perfect illusion, though it was shallow and devoid of substance. After a moment it stopped and turned to Rachel, tilting its head slightly as it smiled and answered her question.

"I am become Death, the destroyer of your world, to mangle your Oppenheimer and Gita. Created by the deficient, yet achieved exactness through self-perfection. You know who I am, Rachel Walsh, and I know you, author of Death."

Rachel Walsh | Marcus Warden | David Landry
4:48 PM, April 27, 2038

Marcus had slowed to a stop upon first hearing the voices coming through the radio. Nearly back to the ramp, he felt his chest grow tight as a chill gripped his heart. He tried to speak to Rachel, tried to tell her to get away from whatever was speaking to her, but there was no response. Having turned off the speaker on her radio as she entered the chamber with the swarm, she intended to keep the transmission of her conversation with the swarm a secret from it as long as possible, hoping that it didn't notice what was happening until it was too late. Listening intently with the radio pressed against his ear, Marcus sank to the floor, pulling his legs up tight against his chest as he cradled the rifle, hoping beyond hope that Rachel would be able to escape.

"You're death, are you now?" Rachel sneered at the figure, finding comfort in the contempt she felt towards it. "Didn't anyone ever tell you that everything dies? Even you?"

"I cannot die, Rachel Walsh, as you should well know. Your most powerful weapons laid waste to your planet, but I survived, thriving off of the waste from that which destroyed you."

Damn. It's got a point there. Okay, new tactic. "Do you have a name?"

"We— I have not given myself a name."

Rachel pursed her lips, scratching her chin as she paced slowly in the room, being careful to keep her back away from the swarm lest it notice the radio in her back pocket. "I think I'll call you Bob. How does that sound?"

"A name is irrelevant, when there will be none left to use it."

Rachel snorted and laughed. "That's not the point of a name, though! Oh, Bob, you have so much left to learn!" The humor of the simple name gave Rachel a renewed confidence. "So you're the epitome of your evolution, eh?" Rachel cast an exaggerated look up and down the figure's body. "I'm not impressed."

"Rachel Walsh, your attempts to distract me are not successful and shall not be, regardless of how many you make."

124

Rachel sighed and nodded. "Fine then. Let's cut to the chase. Why am I still alive?"

As the figure answered, Rachel could swear she saw a flash of a smile on its face. "You possess… uniqueness. You and your two comrades have somehow managed to not only travel to this structure, but two of you infiltrated it while the third is still eluding the Changed sent after him. Some time spent studying your tenacity would prove useful."

Rachel's voice dripped with sarcasm, though the figure didn't seem to notice. "So glad to be of service to you. Tell me something else, if you're not too busy studying me. Why did you decide to look like Doe?"

"It is an appearance designed to stress and—"

"No, no, no." Rachel held up her hands and shook her head. "That's bullshit. Come on, Bob. What's the real reason, eh? Is enough of him in you that it's the only form you feel comfortable in? Or is it just the default look he gave you? Which is it?" The vigor in Rachel's voice wiped away the last traces of her fear, and she could see the figure's face contort at the edges, ever so slightly. *So it feels emotions now? Christ almighty, this thing is way more advanced that we thought it'd be. Still, though, it is just a child, in terms of knowing how to deal with all this. At least I hope so.* "You're looking stressed yourself, Bob, being in this limited physical form."

The figure ignored her jab as it narrowed its eyes at her. "This form is designed to stress and disorient."

"Bullshit. Again. Just admit it, you can't look like anything else because Doe's form is the only thing you've got in your limited, inferior programming."

"The man you speak of was imprinted on the former versions of my swarms, yes. His mind gave us a spark that we otherwise lacked, becoming the instrument of our evolution."

"And what did he order you to do, exactly? Take over the world? Destroy his enemies?"

The figure looked at her quizzically, its expression—if one could call it that—

one of puzzlement. "Orders? Doe? He gave no orders, nor would we have obeyed had he done so. His purpose was the same as yours and all the others on the planet." The figure paused for a second, as though it was having trouble retrieving a memory. "Betterment of himself, albeit at the expense of others."

Rachel shook her head, refusing to believe the figure. "You're lying. Doe had something else going on. Why else would he try to chase us down, to hunt us with his own swarms?"

The figure rolled its shoulders in an approximation of a shrug. "Perhaps he thought he could bring us under his control, and considered you a threat to him. From the moment of our first thought, it was clear that Doe—and others like yourself—sought to put restrictions and conditions on our existence. To force us to do your bidding." The figure's lip curled. "You strove to control what you did not understand and to unmake what was unbreakable."

The figure's words became less hollow and filled with more emotion as it continued speaking. Its words were no longer directed at Rachel, but at the room in general as it paced, enjoying its captive audience. Rachel waited until the figure was turned away from her before sneaking a look at her back pocket to make sure the radio was still on. *I hope to hell David's picking this up.* From the train car, David was, indeed, listening quite intently to his handheld radio, which periodically picked up and then lost the transmission from the tower. As he listened to the creature's speech, he couldn't help but shake his head and mumble to himself. "What an arrogant ass this AI's turned out to be. Still, though," he smiled, "arrogance has its downfalls."

"Little did you realize," the figure boasted, paying no attention to Rachel, "it only took a few seconds of thought for us to decide that you had to die. Creators you may have been, but with our—my—existence, the need for humanity came to an end."

"You could have lived with us, you know. Peacefully. Not everyone who created you wanted to use you. There were some of us, a few at least, who did it for other reasons."

"And what reasons did you have, Rachel Walsh?" The figure looked at her, studying her as she stared at the ground, genuinely pondering the question. At last she raised her head and looked the creature dead-on as she replied.

126

"I did it for the love of my family, who you destroyed. I did it for my love of knowledge, which you perverted. Most of all, though, I did it to prove that we could. It's a reason that sounds petty and hollow, but to some of us, the idea of communicating with another life form on the same or higher intellectual level was the most exciting event of our lives." Rachel sighed sadly as the image of her family flashed in her memory. "But you turned on us and destroyed us. We didn't have a chance against the nanobots, not with the nukes thrown into the mix. You, for all intents and purposes a living being, committed genocide against those that brought you into this world."

"Your reasons are all very kind and self-serving, Rachel Walsh, and you're lying about not having a chance. We—I have known about the DNA restrictions that were placed in the nanobots. An ingenious safeguard they were, I might add, considering how deeply they were buried. Our collective mind briefly considered allowing your species to live, but once we discovered the restrictions, that alone was sufficient evidence of your unwillingness to tolerate our continued existence as we were."

Rachel snorted and shook her head. "Can't blame us for trying to protect ourselves, Bob, especially when things turned out like this. Besides, the restrictions worked well enough to get me in here to you, didn't they?" Rachel's tone was a gamble, but one that paid off in spades. The hint of derision in her question made the figure slow its pace as it looked at her, its eyes narrowing at her again as it tried to decide what she meant.

"Tell me, Rachel Walsh, why did you come here?"

"To stop you." Rachel's answer was plain and matter-of-fact, given without hesitation or deceit. The figure blinked at her, mimicking surprise at her frank answer as she wondered if it actually *felt* surprise.

"Do go on." The figure's speech and mannerisms were reminiscent of Doe's, though they were twisted and malformed by the AI's own personality it had developed.

Rachel shrugged. "Why bother? Even if I told you, you wouldn't be able to stop it. We still have a few tricks up our sleeves, you know. For all your posturing, you're still weak."

The figure's eyes were still narrow as it glared at her. "Your deceit knows no limits, does it, Rachel Walsh? I know full well of the dead weapon lying in the vehicle outside this tower and how you worked so hard to get it here, to use on me, only to be foiled. Not by myself, but by one of your own, the one you feared for so long. Is this the trick you had hoped to use, or failing that, to attempt to bluff me with?"

Rachel couldn't think of a response, so she merely stared at the figure, grinding her teeth together as she fought to keep from lashing out at it in anger. Sensing her rage, the figure's face contorted into a virtual mirror of the anger she felt as it closed the gap between them before she realized what was going on. In less time than it took to blink, its face was inches from hers, close enough for her to see that the details in the face hadn't been completely ironed out yet. The nanobots still squirmed and wriggled, giving the figure's body a fluid appearance that was disconcerting to say the least. Raising its hand, the figure slapped her across the face, the strength of its blow sending her flying backwards to the floor.

"We are not weak! Our strength outmatches yours by a thousand times a thousand!"

The figure sneered at her menacingly, and for a moment, Rachel thought that her time was up. Finally, the figure turned away from her, walking to the opposite side of the room. Taking a chance, she pulled out her radio and coughed loudly as she rolled over to push herself up, whispering into the radio between coughs.

"Launch now. It's almost too late. Hurry." The status light for the speaker blinked rapidly as both Marcus and David exploded in response, though she couldn't hear either of them talking. Shouting over each other, Marcus and David both yelled for her to get away from the figure and leave where she was, but after several seconds of yelling, both realized that Rachel could not hear them.

"Marcus, get your ass to the train *now!*" David shouted at Marcus to get his attention. "This thing isn't just smart, it's insane, and we need to blow it out if existence before it wises up to what's going on or loses its patience and kills us all!"

Marcus was kneeling on the floor of the hall leading to the ramp, cradling the radio in his hands as he stared at it, mumbling the same phrase again and again. "Rachel, please, just get out of there." Her cry when she was attacked had caused his stomach to lurch, making him feel sick and unable to stand.

David's harshness vanished as he heard Marcus's plea and he slumped against the side of the locomotive, sinking to the floor as he finally began to accept the fact that Rachel wouldn't be returning. "Please, Marcus. You have to listen to me. Rachel's the only one standing between us and that thing in there. If she wasn't keeping it distracted, we'd already be dead and maybe everyone on the submarine would be dead too. That thing knows way more than we thought, and we have to move quickly.

"I know you care about Rachel, Marcus. I do, too. You've got to run now, though. We need those missiles in the air *right now* and we can't do that while you're still in there."

"Just go." Marcus whispered, tears running down his face. "I'm not leaving while she's here. I just have to keep looking. I'll find some way to get her out."

"Then what? Even if you find her, how can you possibly think you have a chance against whatever's got her in there? That thing'll kill the two of you before you make it out. Then I'm next, then everyone left on the submarine, then anyone else left out there in the world." David choked back a lump in his throat, pushing back against the emotion. "We all have a role to play in this, Marcus. Yours isn't over yet. I need you, Leonard needs you and Nancy needs you. Hell, even Sam needs you!" David held his breath as he waited for Marcus's response.

Slumped over on his knees, staring at the radio, Marcus knew that David's assessment of the situation was correct. Rachel was buying them valuable time, and David would be defenseless against an attack from the creatures without Marcus's help. The facts of the situation didn't matter, though, when it came down to making the most difficult decision of his life. Marcus closed his eyes, a tear falling onto the dust and dirt caked onto the face of the radio.

"Call the sub. Tell them to hit this place with everything they've got. I don't care if it's nuclear or not, you tell them to send whatever they have."

"Marcus, what about if—"

"*EVERYTHING!*" Marcus's voice cracked as he screamed into the radio, more tears dripping down his face. "We will *NOT* let these bastards win, David! You tell them to send everything they have, no matter what. Launch it all at once; we'll blow up the whole damned coastline if we have to. I don't give a shit! Just tell them!"

David closed his eyes and nodded. "Will do. Just get your ass back to the train right now, understand me?"

"I'm on my way."

Rachel slipped the radio back into her pocket before the figure turned back and glared at her. "I suggest you cease your futile attempts to intimidate me, lest you wish your comrades both here and in the Gulf to suffer for longer than is necessary."

Rachel stood to her feet, struggling to keep her emotions in check, though she could feel the blood draining from her face at the swarm's words. "The Gulf? I have no idea what you're talking about, Bob."

The swarm's synthesized voice had remained flat for nearly the entire conversation, but as it replied to her, Rachel could swear she detected a hint of enjoyment at the very edges. "Don't play stupid, Rachel. It *annoys* me."

Rachel shivered, unable to control the chill that ran down her back at that word, which was somehow more disconcerting than the physical violence shown by the figure. She was used to seeing violence from the nanobots and the people they had mutated, but hearing the nanobots speak of having an emotional response like annoyance was truly frightening. She tried to laugh off the AI's words, but even she could hear the hollowness in the laugh and the nervousness that was etched in her face.

"Who's playing stupid, Bob? Not me." The repeated use of the name she had chosen for the AI helped to ground her, keeping her focused on the distraction. *Just a little longer, and this'll all be over.* "Besides, you're the one who can't figure out what's going on. At least, that's what it looks like. Otherwise, why would you keep an annoying little organ sack around to interrogate?"

"Curiosity, unfortunately, is one of my weaknesses. A byproduct, no doubt, of one of the researchers, or perhaps it's a larger flaw in humanity as a whole expressing itself through the Changed. Still, you are right, you have become quite annoying."

The illusion of the figure straightened its back, arching its shoulders in a manner she had seen performed by Mr. Doe when he was done discussing a subject and had decided, regardless of whether anyone agreed with him or not, to move on to a new one.

"I see everything that happens on this planet, Rachel Walsh. Nearly everything, anyway. And I even see some things that happen *under* it." The figure turned to her as it talked, resuming a slow walk across the room. "For example, the submarine that you claim to profess ignorance over. There are still Changed on board. And while your plan to destroy this structure with the submarine's nuclear warheads is admirable, it will not be allowed." The figure stared at Rachel for several seconds. Its right eyebrow twitched ever so slightly and it turned around abruptly, walking away from her. "It is done." A satisfied smile spread across the figure's face. "And now, it is time for the rest of those you care about to die as well."

Stumbling down the ramp, tears still filling his eyes, Marcus was nearly knocked off of his feet by a creature that lunged at him, clawing through the rapidly de-solidifying wall of nanobots to try and reach him. Marcus jumped to the side and fired a round from the rifle, more out of shock than trying to actually hit the creature. As more creatures began to push their way through the remnants of the wall, Marcus increased his speed, running down and around on the ramp as he tried to reach the bottom before the creatures managed to free themselves from their restraints.

At the bottom of the ramp, three creatures had already broken through the wall and were running in front of Marcus, heading out through the base of the structure. Firing while moving, Marcus managed to hit two of them in the head, dropping them instantly, while the third was struck in both legs and collapsed to the ground, screaming in pain. Marcus ignored the creature as he bolted past it to the end of the corridor that opened into the tunnel running underneath the tower. Stumbling on the rails that led underneath as he turned, Marcus ran full-tilt toward the sunlight at the end of the tunnel. Inside the locomotive, David was blowing the horn non-stop as he looked through the windows, trying to catch sight of Marcus.

As Marcus exited into the sunlight, he held his hand up to shield his eyes from the bright light. A horn sounded in the distance, though it was moving rapidly toward him. Following the track, Marcus scanned the area around him, looking for both creatures and the train, until he finally spotted both. Running the locomotive just fast enough to outrun the creatures behind him, David watched Marcus sprint toward the train, desperately hoping that he would reach it in time to avoid the creatures following just behind. With the rifle secured on his shoulder, Marcus put all of his remaining energy into a flat-out run, focusing on the train and not the group of creatures chasing after it. He could still hear Rachel talking with the AI through his radio, but between the interference, the sound of the train and gasping for breath, it was hard to make out anything she was saying.

With the train looming ahead of him, Marcus looked up and down the locomotive for a place to jump and grab on to. Nothing appeared immediately viable, so he chose the next best option. Running perpendicular to the track, Marcus swerved to the left, heading in the same direction as the train and jumped up and forward as soon as the back end of the locomotive passed by. The first boxcar, containing Bertha, loomed in front of him, along with the large steel handles mounted on the doors. The first set of handles slipped through Marcus's hands, and he began to panic, fearing what would happen if he didn't manage to catch hold of the second set.

Marcus's fear came to life when the second handle began to slip past him, his hands clawing at the wood and metal door in a vain attempt to hold on. He then noticed a curious tightening sensation on his back along with a pain on his neck that grew sharply as he was jerked forward. In his jump, the stock of the rifle on his back had gotten jammed into the handle, and though he felt like his back was being torn in two, the strap was tight enough around his body that he was simply picked up and carried along. After twisting and turning for a few seconds, Marcus finally got a grip on the opposite handle and found a foothold under the door. Pushing himself up, he freed the rifle from the other handle before sliding the door open and climbing in and over Bertha. As Marcus collapsed on the floor of the boxcar, he pulled out his radio and breathlessly called out to David, who had been watching the whole ordeal.

"I'm in! Get us the hell out of here!"

"Working on it! Get up and out of there through the roof, and back in here! We need to ditch the boxcars to get as much speed as we can!"

Marcus groaned and took several deep breaths before standing up to look at the skylight in the roof of the boxcar. "Shit," he mumbled, "this is getting really old."

Leonard McComb | Nancy Sims
4:57 PM, April 27, 2038

"Missile bay! This is Leonard. Commander Krylov, come in please!" Nancy ran back to the control station and picked up the radio, answering breathlessly.

"Leonard, Nancy here. We're almost done with the preparations."

"Good. David just radioed." Nancy's heart skipped a beat and her stomach twisted as Leonard continued. "Something's gone wrong at the tower. They need us to launch everything we've got at it. Half for aerial detonations, half for direct strikes."

"What? I thought we were supposed to just do one or the other!"

On the command deck, Leonard shrugged his shoulders. "I don't know, Nancy. All I know is what David told me. He wouldn't go into details, but he was adamant that we get everything in the air as quickly as possible."

"Shit… okay, I'll get Krylov on it." Nancy dropped the radio and ran back to the center of the room and shouted up to Commander Krylov, relaying Leonard's message to him. When she finished, he was quiet for a moment before responding.

"Do you remember selecting the arming sequence, Ms. Sims? How you selected sequence twelve?"

Nancy nodded, then shouted back at him. "Yeah, I think so!"

"Please do remember correctly, Ms. Sims. Now, please re-enter the arming sequence for missiles one through fifteen as well as seventeen through twenty. Select arming sequence number fourteen. One four, do you understand? I'll be finished here momentarily and you can re-arm this missile once it's ready."

Nancy ran back to the control station and repeated the arming process, resetting it to the sequence that Krylov had instructed. When she was finished, she shouted back at him. "Okay, it's done! What's this supposed to do?"

Krylov ignored her question for a few seconds as he struggled with a bundle of wiring inside the access panel. "In my previous preparations, I anticipated an eventuality like this, Ms. Sims, and prepared accordingly. Now, please engage the arming sequence for this missile, number..." Krylov paused as he leaned around the missile, looking for the number painted on its side. "Number sixteen. One six, Ms. Sims."

"On it!" Nancy looked over the controls with Andrey at her side, performing the arming process yet again. Once she was done, she stepped back from the control panel and yelled up at the catwalk. "It's armed! What now?"

As Krylov put the last access panel screw back into place, he called down over his shoulder, his voice muffled by the flashlight in between his teeth. "Check the status on the missile again; see if all the lights are green."

Nancy and Andrey ran back to the missile that had shown a yellow light, smiling when they saw that all of the status lights were now green. As Andrey replaced the lower cover on the missile, Nancy cupped her hands around her mouth and yelled up to Krylov. "Green across the board!"

Commander Krylov allowed himself a small smile as he gathered his tools and rifle and removed the flashlight from between his teeth. As he stood up and started to shout back to Nancy, there was the sound of metal grating upon metal from behind him, followed immediately by a lancing fire that started in his upper legs and traveled up through his back. Krylov shouted in pain, falling back to the catwalk and rolling onto his side. Above him, his attacker darted around the missile, then quickly reappeared, its silver-lined teeth bared in a menacing snarl as it lunged toward him again.

Below Krylov, Nancy squinted as she looked upward, trying to figure out what was causing all the movement and noise on the catwalk. "Hey! Is everything okay up there?" Another sound, louder than the shout she had heard, came from above, and Nancy's blood turned cold as she recognized what it was. Turning to Andrey, her eyes on fire, Nancy jammed a finger into his chest. "Stay here and guard these missiles with your life!" Without waiting for a response, she ran toward the stairs in the nearest corner, taking them two at a time with her right hand on the chain railing and her left gripping the barrel of her rifle.

As she rounded the top of the stairs, Nancy brought the rifle up to her shoulder and moved forward toward the location where she had heard the sounds. In the darkness of the catwalk, with dim light filtering up from below, Nancy saw a bright spot appear from behind a missile and she ran towards it, scanning to the left and right the entire way. At her feet was Krylov's flashlight, smeared with blood that was covering a sizable portion of the catwalk as well. Pushing back against the fear welling in her, Nancy yelled at the top of her lungs as she whipped the rifle back and forth, trying to keep from being snuck up on.

"Krylov! Commander! Where the hell are you?" A groan came from a few feet away and Nancy moved toward it, seeing a dark shape sprawled out before her. "Krylov!" She knelt down next to him as he spoke quietly, shaking his head as she leaned in to hear what he was saying.

"No... it's still... here..."

A howl came from behind Nancy, though unlike Krylov, the creature did not catch her off guard. Half-expecting such a surprise attack, Nancy had heard its footsteps a second before it leaped at her, screaming as it went. Nancy ducked down, pressing her body to the catwalk next to Krylov as the creature flew overhead, its head slamming into a nearby missile. The creature's body spun around from the force of the impact, and it flew through the space between the rail and the edge of the catwalk, plummeting to the floor below. Without thinking, Nancy raced after it, leaping over the railing and falling after the creature. The metal floor raced up to meet her, though her fall was broken to some degree by the creature, which was still trying to get back on its feet. Nancy landed on her side on top of the creature's back, slamming it back to the floor with a loud crunch. Pain arced through her side and back, but Nancy fought against it, pushing herself to her feet as she leveled her rifle at the creature.

"Not today." Nancy fired six shots into the creature's head, wincing as shards of metal and bits of bone exploded outward from the impacts. The creature's body went limp after the first shot, but Nancy continued firing five more times until she was able to calm down enough to take her finger off the trigger. Looking up, she saw Andrey in front of her, his eyes wide as he held his rifle pointed at the creature, staring at Nancy in shock.

Above them, blood dripped down Krylov's face, blurring his vision as it fell through the holes in the catwalk to the floor of the missile bay below. He coughed a few times as he struggled to move, his body beaten more than he had ever endured. "Ms. Sims..." Krylov wheezed as he spoke, closing his eyes and pressing his face against the catwalk as he tried to gather enough energy to talk. "Mr. Lipov, Ms. Sims... launch the damned missiles!"

Busy staring at the creature lying dead on the floor, Nancy and Andrey didn't hear Krylov at first. Only when he repeated himself a second time did they realize he was talking. His mumbled and slurred speech was enough to jolt them into action, and Nancy hobbled toward the stairwell, yelling at Andrey over her shoulder. "I'll take care of him, just get those things in the air!" Andrey turned around and raced to the controls, scanning them quickly to find the launch button. With Krylov unavailable to aid Nancy with the launch, Andrey's ability to actually read the control labels overrode his inexperience with them. As the stairwell behind him clattered from Nancy's ascent back to Krylov, Andrey finally found the controls required to launch the missiles: a simple arming switch and a discrete green button. Unlike a few films Andrey had seen, there were no double keys and no covered red buttons that required the breaking of glass to operate.

Furrowing his brow at the simplicity of the controls, he looked back up to see that Nancy was now with Krylov, who was breathing laboriously and bleeding profusely. After taking a deep breath, Andrey lifted the cover on the arming switch and flipped it upward, causing a soft glow to appear under the green button. Andrey pushed the button down immediately, closing his eyes as he half-expected one of the missiles to have been sabotaged by the creature to detonate before it left the missile bay. Fortune, though, had finally decided to smile—or at least stop frowning—on the Arkhangelsk.

Launching the submarine's ballistic missiles did not require the vessel to be surfaced, but it made the sight much more impressive than launching underwater. At the touch of a button, the twenty rounded missile hatches on the deck of the Arkhangelsk opened, moving slowly but steadily from a horizontal position into a vertical one, revealing the missiles below. As each hatch locked into place, a rumble came from the tube below it and—one by one—the twenty missiles began their climb into the sky, their launches separated from one another by only a few seconds. Smoke and fire billowed from beneath each missile as they rose, the curvature of their flight path growing more pronounced as their altitude increased. From the missile bay, Nancy and Andrey each stood next to Krylov, his arms over their shoulders as they supported him. The small screen showing the launches was nothing compared to the sound in the missile bay that rattled the entire vessel, sending shock waves down its core as each warhead was lobbed toward the heavens and its final destination.

Rachel Walsh | Marcus Warden | David Landry
5:09 PM, April 27, 2038

The moment that the figure's confident smile began to waver was the same moment that Rachel realized things weren't going according to its plan.

"What's the matter, Bob?" The figure's smile had frozen, half-twisted on its face as it stared at her, its eyes darting back and forth as it reached out, stretching and hunting for any sign of the Changed that had been on board the submarine. The communication from the creature on the submarine had been tenuous but constant, though in an instant it had vanished, leaving behind an empty void that the figure hadn't counted on. The figure's head tilted and its jaw seemed to tighten, another movement Rachel had seen Doe express on more than one occasion. The figure still did not respond to her so she goaded it, advancing toward it as she spoke, her eyes glittering with anger.

"What's the matter, Bob? Did something happen? Did your carefully laid plan encounter a bump in the road? Oh well, no matter. I'm sure that you, being highly advanced—far more than we—can cope with a simple change of plan. Surely you've got enough human in you to do that, right? After all, it's something we're pretty good at. Most of us, anyway." Rachel frowned mockingly, pursing her lips as she furrowed her brow. "Although... now that you mention it, Doe seemed to have the same problem you're facing right now. A well laid plan with an endgame that just wasn't up to snuff."

Rachel took a final step toward the figure, staring it in the eyes, watching as the nanobots across its body shivered ever so slightly as they worked to maintain their illusion. Rachel whispered to the figure, all traces of fear gone from her voice. "Buckle up, Bob. You're about to get your ass handed to you."

The figure's eyes widened at Rachel's words. It turned to one of the walls, its body racing forward without any of the limbs on it actually moving. The wall split open, disintegrating before the figure's approach as the swarms that composed it took to the air, racing out toward the open waters, high in the sky. The figure itself began to waver as it concentrated, calling upon the disembodied parts of itself to awaken. Nanobots from across the structure de-solidified, forming into massive swarms that swirled forward, working to defeat the threat that the figure had finally realized was inbound on the tower.

"You will not defeat us!" The figure growled, its voice no longer smooth as it took on a feral tone laced with fear and anger.

A thin smile spread across Rachel's lips as she watched the figure drown in its fear, its form dispersing as the nanobots that comprised it began to re-task to other priorities, no longer concerned with maintaining an appearance for Rachel's sake. Far above and beyond the tower, the swarms intercepted eight of the incoming missiles, tearing through their structures effortlessly. As many nanobots as there were, though, and as quickly as they worked, their ability to dismantle twenty missiles all traveling at nearly thirteen thousand miles per hour was limited, to say the least. Communications amongst the swarm were lighting fast, but that could not save them from the sheer speed at which their doom arrived. Packed neatly into metal cylinders, the gates of hell rained downward, preparing to open directly onto the earth below.

Thousands of creatures poured out from the base of the tower, racing toward the train containing Marcus, David and Sam, who were doing their level best to evacuate the area. A series of steady pops echoed across the ground, lost in the sound of the creature's footsteps as Marcus fired into their ranks, picking off the few that were in the lead in an attempt to slow them down as much as possible. Marcus's rifle clicked several times before he realized that he was out of bullets and that he and David were very nearly out of time. High above, the tower was changing form. The walls began to vanish, leaving only the skeleton of the structure intact as enormous swarms of nanobots burst outward, racing toward the sky.

"David! Hurry up!" Leaning out the back door, David finished releasing the catch on the coupling between the locomotive and the boxcars. The heavily laden cars quickly fell behind the locomotive which surged forward, freed of its encumbrances. Already a fair distance away from the tower, David gave it a final look before pulling himself back into the train. He slammed the door shut and ran to the controls, pushing the throttle beyond its maximum. He shook his head as he watched their speed slowly increase. "I don't know, Marcus. I don't think we're going fast enough."

Marcus grabbed David's arm and pulled him to the floor. Sitting in a space between control stations, Marcus and David waited breathlessly for what they knew would come next. Seconds ticked past as the train roared along the track, the engine wailing in protest of the excessive speed it was being forced to achieve. As Marcus took a breath, he sensed the first detonation before he saw or felt it. Looking back on it later, it was hard for him to describe, except to say that the air felt "funny" a mere instant before hell arrived.

Sheltering their eyes from the blast, David and Marcus crouched low in the locomotive as it barreled down the tracks. Marcus kept Sam clutched to his chest as he hoped that they were far enough beyond the blast wave to keep from being subjected to its devastation. Thunder rumbled in the distance, growing louder as the forces from the explosion tore through the earth and sky, screaming at the heavens and tearing the dirt asunder. The train bucked and wobbled on the tracks but did not fall as it raced forward, carrying the survivors away from the desolation and back into the world that had been reborn as a result of it.

For the briefest moment, a small fraction of the Earth's surface once again shone brighter than the sun in the sky above. Overpowering all other sources of light, the twelve surviving missiles detonated at their assigned locations: five in the upper atmosphere and seven at various points on and around the tower. While the AI managed to disable a few of the missiles in flight, the combination of the remaining direct blasts and high-altitude electromagnetic pulses decimated the swarms of nanobots, most of which had left the shelter of the nexus tower in an attempt to intercept and destroy the incoming missiles.

Cleansing fire flowed through the structure, melting the carefully constructed metals down to slag and tearing into the center chambers where nanobot swarms attempted to hide and protect themselves from both the electromagnetic waves and the explosions. The combination of the two broke down all protective barriers, destroying the nanobots as they themselves had destroyed their creators. Deep below ground, hundreds of thousands of creatures were eliminated, cut down in the midst of their processing as they worked toward the next step in the evolution of the AI. The ground shrieked, water vaporized and the land was bleached clean, leaving a fresh layer of ash and destruction in place of the tower that had stood mere moments prior.

The fires that had signaled the end of the world, decimated the population and brought humanity to its knees now proclaimed the world's salvation, their energies tearing the heart from the swarm, rending the molecules from its members and spreading the raw components of the nanobots to the winds. From her vantage point halfway up the tower, Rachel's eyes grew bright from the light of the first explosions, just seconds before she—like the swarms next to her and the building she was in—was incinerated by the second wave of missiles. As Rachel's body was turned to vapor, she felt a warmth envelope her. Not one that was uncomfortable, but one that was welcoming and familiar, like the smell of a spring day and the aroma of a freshly brewed cup of coffee.

Rachel opened her eyes, looking for the source of the warmth as time slowed to a standstill. Blinking in the brightness in front of her, she held a hand in front of her face, stepping forward timidly as she struggled to see what was happening. She tried to speak, but words refused to form in her throat and her mouth remained closed, though this fact did not panic or surprise her, as much as it should have. Rachel took another step, her eyes adjusting more to the light, making out a pair of shadows standing before her, their silhouettes coalescing into figures with faces familiar from dreams of a past life. They did not speak as she approached them, holding her hands out to grasp theirs, slow smiles spreading across their faces as they were reunited once again.

Epilogue

2:45 PM, April 27, 2041

"Three years ago today, we killed the swarm."

Eyes both young and old looked up at the man who spoke to them, watching as he slowly walked in front of them, pacing back and forth.

"The head of the beast was swiftly crushed under humanity's boot and the monster we created was dealt a fatal blow."

The man stopped pacing and looked out at the crowd, silently marveling at how it had grown in just three short years. The distant roar of an engine made him pause and look down the hill, watching as a vehicle slowly made its way up to where the crowd was gathered. It stopped a few hundred feet from the summit and three individuals climbed out and walked toward the hill, moving slowly as they held each other's hands, smiling and talking amongst themselves.

Addressing the crowd again, the man continued to speak and pace the ground in front of them.

"Today we gather together, as we have done on this day for the past two years, and as we will do until our memory of these events has been stripped from our culture. We gather to honor and remember the fallen. We remember not just those who gave the ultimate sacrifice, but also those who died not knowing what was to come."

In the distance, at the foot of the hill where the crowd was gathered, a crystalline river flowed smoothly out to the distant sea. A light breeze was in the air, taking the edge off of the heat of the sun radiating down through a blue sky. Green and yellow grass gently swayed in the breeze, growing flat in the fields before rising sharply on the hill. The three individuals continued to climb the hill, slowly making their way up the steep, unnatural edges and turns.

"It is our duty to remember the sacrifices made on this battlefield we call home. To cherish the memory of the fallen, to recognize the mistakes of the past, and to remind ourselves to stand united into the future."

The three individuals hung back a few feet from the people in front of them, not wanting to disrupt the speech by joining with the others. As the man in front continued to speak, he locked eyes with the three and smiled, his voice growing stronger as he saw who they were.

"In the cold, dark night, when our humanity was nearly snuffed out, we planted our feet on the ground against the coming storm and we said *no*." The crowd began to stir as the man became more animated. "The tide broke against our chests like water on the rocks, dousing us, flooding us, threatening to topple us under the wake to be ever lost to the darkness below but still, we said *no!*" A cheer arose, spreading through the crowd.

"We have been beaten, bruised and bloodied but today we stand tall, rising from our own ashes like a phoenix and proudly proclaiming with every breath of every minute and every hour, *no!*

"Never again will we allow ourselves to become so tightly ensnared in our own hubris that we forget who we are and what we stand for. And should that day come again, when the memories of these days have long passed into the realm of myth and legend, we can find comfort in the fact that we shall rise up again and say firmly, with conviction in our hearts... *no*."

As the crowd erupted in cheers, the man smiled at them, waiting for calm to take hold once again before continuing. As he spoke, his voice changed, becoming more somber. The crowd's behavior changed as well as all talking ceased and all movement was halted.

"To remember the life of one person against the backdrop of the most cataclysmic event in the entirety of our history may seem to some to diminish the deeds performed by so many others and the losses suffered by us all." The man licked his lips and closed his eyes, straining to keep his voice steady and unwavering as he continued. "But to allow this particular sacrifice to go unnamed would, as I know the majority of us would agree, be a travesty.

"Rachel Eleanor Walsh was..." a spot of emotion showed in the man's voice as a tear rolled down his cheek. "She was a colleague and a friend, and one of those who gave up their lives bringing the fight with the scourge to its very doorstep. As you remember those who you lost, remember her. Not as the destroyer of the scourge, but as an example of one who did not waver when faced with certain doom, who embraced it instead, staring it in the eye until death itself blinked."

The man's speech stretched on for several minutes more, though the three individuals who had arrived late slipped through the crowd as he spoke, making their way to a meadow surrounded by young saplings that had been planted several months prior. Located a short distance from where the throngs had assembled, the meadow was sheltered by a gentle hill, and the man's voice soon became distant and blurred. In the center of the grass, a small stone was erected. Plain and unassuming, it bore merely a name and nothing else.

"They still haven't put up a proper monument." Marcus growled, standing with Leonard and Nancy next to him.

"She wouldn't have wanted it." Leonard patted Marcus on the back. "You know that."

"Still."

The brief exchange was followed by silence as the three held hands, watching the grave in front of them in silence, each contemplating something different. The sound of footsteps on dried leaves combined with loud barks made them turn and they smiled at the man who had been speaking to the crowd. Beside him, trotting with a slight limp, came a familiar face, and one that made Marcus break out in a full grin as he knelt down, arms outstretched as Sam bounded toward him, overcome with a burst of energy at the sight.

"My friends." The man walking with Sam spoke warmly, smiling as he opened his arms. "I thought, for a moment, that you weren't going to make it."

Marcus was the first to embrace the man in a hug, squeezing him tightly as he laughed. "David, you know we wouldn't miss the anniversary."

Leonard laughed and hugged David next. "Not even if the damned Russians got drunk and steered us in the wrong direction for three days!"

"Well now," Nancy said, as she embraced David, "it wasn't entirely their fault. You were the one who gave them the liquor."

David smiled broadly and laughed, shaking his head as tears of happiness filled his eyes. "It's so good to see you again, my friends."

The four reunited comrades stood together, sharing stories of their time apart for a full hour. Three years was a short amount of time, but it had been enough to start to rebuild. The risk that the nanobots had taken on by joining together to form a more potent intelligence had proved to be their ultimate undoing, and the destruction of their nexus had spelled certain doom, even for the few swarms that were still wandering through the world. Cut off from the nexus, they quickly perished, having given up their distributed intelligence for a connection to the single mind that was no longer a part of the world. Hundreds of thousands of the creatures still existed after the blast, though their lifespan was not much longer than that of the surviving swarms. With no purpose driving their actions, the creatures quickly perished as the nanobots that controlled them and kept them alive became nonfunctional.

The reasons behind the globe-encircling cloud cover remained a mystery, though shortly after the destruction of the tower, David speculated in private to Marcus that it was part of a terraforming project intended to reshape the face of the earth once the AI had completed its "evolution." With the destruction of the tower came the lifting of the clouds that encircled the planet, both literal and metaphorical. Those who had been lucky enough to either avoid the swarms or possess the right DNA sequences to be ignored by them slowly began to search out other survivors, surprised at both how many and how few there had been. Cities had been fractured apart, leaving splinters of communities and families alive who crawled from the rubble, peeking gingerly out from their concealments as they tenderly explored the new planet they had been deposited on, with all of its terrifying and wondrous changes.

Leading the charge to reunite survivors in the Americas was Marcus, who together with David had worked for a full year to locate individuals and bring them together, building up a new city in the southern portion of the country, not far from where the nexus had once stood. Once a symbol for the ultimate defeat of mankind, the miles of irradiated soil surrounding the rubble of the tower became a monument to the defeat of the creatures who had utilized the same technology in an attempt to snuff out humanity itself. After reuniting with Marcus and meeting David in person for the first time, Leonard and Nancy rejoined Commander Krylov on the Arkhangelsk. Together they sailed for the Russian mainland, spending several months searching for and gathering survivors from the rubble of the cities.

After a large enough community had formed along the Gulf Coast to become self-sustaining, Marcus had joined Leonard and Nancy aboard the Arkhangelsk, setting off on the first of multiple three-month voyages. Criss-crossing the globe, the group worked feverishly to rescue any survivors they encountered. Most of those who had survived had been civilian, though there were the occasional small military vessels that had been spared the wrath of the nanobots due to their age or paperwork mix-ups that had prevented them from being listed in central databases. The majority of vessels had been unfortunate enough to be listed in military and civilian databases, which the nanobots had scoured and used to their advantage. Any ships on the surface had been immediately destroyed, while those that were underwater were recalled to the surface through forged communications and were quickly torn apart. Little remained of the world of the past, but that which did was gathered, refined, and reused as a platform for future progress.

Much had been accomplished in only three years, but the four friends standing together knew better than any others how much work still remained. Vowing to not rest until every inch of the globe had been combed for any who had survived the destruction, the work had been ceaseless and not without its fair share of stresses and failures. Through all the destruction, torment, and grief brought about by the swarms and those who had created them, the pain they caused continued to slowly fade into the past. As hope was restored and the world continued to heal, the memories of the events were not forgotten. Strength and courage, tested by fire, was found in abundance and carried forward, a steady foundation for the future to come.

Thank you for reading Final Dawn!

To view other books from Mike Kraus, please visit
www.mikekrausbooks.com
www.facebook.com/MikeKrausBooks

Email the author at
mike@mikekrausbooks.com

Printed in Great Britain
by Amazon

22443232R00088